COLUMBIA PICTURES AND CASTLE ROCK ENTERTAINMENT PRESENT
AN APPLE/ROSE PRODUCTION A WOLFGANG PETERSEN FILM
CLINT EASTWOOD   JOHN MALKOVICH   RENE RUSSO

"IN THE LINE OF FIRE"

DYLAN McDERMOTT   GARY COLE
FRED DALTON THOMPSON AND JOHN MAHONEY
MUSIC COMPOSED BY ENNIO MORRICONE   WRITTEN BY JEFF MAGUIRE
CO-PRODUCED BY BOB ROSENTHAL
EXECUTIVE PRODUCERS WOLFGANG PETERSEN   GAIL KATZ AND DAVID VALDES
PRODUCED BY JEFF APPLE

DIRECTED BY WOLFGANG PETERSEN

IN THE LINE OF FIRE

A novel by Max Allan Collins
Based on the screenplay written by Jeff Maguire

▰ HarperCollins*Publishers*

HarperCollins*Publishers*
77–85 Fulham Palace Road,
Hammersmith, London W6 8JB

A Paperback Original 1993
1 3 5 7 9 8 6 4 2

A catalogue record for this book
is available from the British Library

ISBN 0 00 647856 5

Set in Aster

Printed in Great Britain by
HarperCollinsManufacturing Glasgow

For Jim Hoffmann—
who mastered the "stare" long ago

"If someone is willing to trade his life for mine there is nothing anyone can do about it."
—PRESIDENT JOHN F. KENNEDY

1

· ·

The dream was always the same.

Hot but beautiful day in Dallas; gliding along, riding the running board of the follow-up car. Nervous—so many people in Texas hated the President—and there the Man was, just up ahead, smiling, waving, lovely wife doing the same, radiant . . .

The President and the First Lady. But they were in black and white. And so was he.

Gliding along, like in a newsreel, an ancient newsreel he'd been spliced into, he was doing his job, watching the crowd, looking for the blank or hostile faces or any suspicious movement or sound, and then there *was* one, a suspicious, sudden sound; but it was just a firecracker.

Wasn't it?

And as he rode the running board, he turned, stuck in the slowest of slow motion, and looked up toward the limo where the President was slumping—*was he hit?*

Christ, the President *was* hit!

But the shock of it froze Secret Service Agent Frank Horrigan; it froze him and he watched in wide-eyed, open-mouthed horror as the President's head exploded into a nightmarish cloudburst of blood and brain and bone, only the bloody burst wasn't in black and white, but color, vivid, horrible Zapruder color. . . .

And Frank Horrigan, as he had so many times over these past decades, sat straight up in bed, sweating, wide-eyed, panting, afraid.

Ashamed.

He heard that a lot of people dreamed in black and white, but this dream was the only black and white one he ever had—and it was interrupted, always, by that awful color burst. There had been a time when he had the dream every night. Now it came almost rarely. Every few months.

But perhaps it had been easier to deal with when it was constant.

He switched on the nightstand lamp, and it blinded him, as always, like the flashbulbs of reporters crowding the Presidents he'd guarded. On the nightstand by his bed were two photos, one of them almost as old as the memory that sparked the recurring dream he'd just woken from.

As if the gesture would steady him or bring him back to reality, he touched the well-worn wooden frame of the photo, an enlarged snapshot he'd taken at a picnic at a state park. Captured there, with glowing smiles, were his beautiful dark-haired wife and his equally lovely dark-haired daughter, who was five when the picture was taken. The other picture on the nightstand was of that same daughter, a grown woman now, still lovely if a little chubby, with her husband, Harold. *And here I am*, he thought, *still playing cops and robbers.*

But it was all he had. That and his piano playing, and he'd never make a living at the latter. Of course he might die at the former, but was that all bad?

He knew he wouldn't be able to sleep, not now, not for a while, and, in just pajama bottoms that were sweated out from the nightmare, he rose—his tanned body looking both younger and older than his years, lean and muscular but scarred, some of it from bullets.

But not a bullet in Dallas. He hadn't taken a bullet that day. If he had, perhaps this country he'd been in the business of protecting for so many years would still have been worth protecting. Of course, in that case, he wouldn't have been alive to know.

Not that he particularly gave a damn.

He wandered into his little living room—the one-bedroom apartment on K street was an untidy, masculine affair—but even in the near dark, Horrigan could skirt the piles of CDs, sheet music and audiophile magazines to find his way to the only possession he truly prized, his Onkyo stereo. He popped Miles Davis's album *Kind of Blue* into the CD player and let its waves of mood wash over him.

Chill him out.

He sighed, still trying to shake the dream, as he went to the little liquor cart and poured himself an inch or two of Jameson Irish Whiskey. He sat on the sofa near the window where a September breeze blew the sheer curtains, making lazy ghosts of them. He looked out onto a street left wet and slick and reflective by a light rain; the reflection of streetlights pooled there.

Frank Horrigan had been handsome, once. He still was, in a craggy, weathered way; but he wasn't the kind of man who cared about his looks. Every year was etched in the narrow-eyed, high-cheekboned mask, a mask that would have been impenetrable had those lines not given away the sorrow and regrets behind it. His hair was thinner. His patience shorter.

Earlier, as on so many evenings, he had dropped by the bar down the street where they would let him sit in the corner and noodle at their piano. He didn't get paid anything for it, of course. He wasn't really good enough to rate payment; but for free, he had a gig whenever he wanted.

Now, in his apartment, he sipped the whiskey, savoring its smoky warmth. When he was finished, he didn't allow himself any more. He'd had a similar amount at the bar, and halted himself. Even after all these years, he could still hear his ex-wife's voice intoning those ominous words: "Drinking problem."

So he didn't have one anymore. In his line of work, in his line of duty, in the line of fire as he was, you goddamn well better not have a drinking problem.

When he went back to bed, the bluesy, jazzy tones of Miles Davis were filtering in from the living room; the warmth of whiskey, and the horn of Miles, were enough to soothe him.

He went to sleep, and slept soundly. The dream did not return.

Not that night.

Mitchell Leary—Mitch to his friends, few of whom were currently alive—had a deceptively gentle smile, but his nearly bald head, high cheekbones and small chin made him look like a grinning skull.

He was grinning that way now, in the cell-like bedroom of his apartment in a rundown building in a seedy section of Washington, D.C., as he Scotch-taped a photo of the President of the United States to a wall littered with many other taped-up photos of the nation's current Commander in Chief.

Some of the photos were clipped from magazines or papers—from the past few State of the Union addresses, of the President waving as he and the First Lady stepped down out of Air Force One. Others were eight-by-ten blowups of shots that Leary had taken himself, from crowds at such events as the Inauguration and at appearances the President had made over the past several months, along the campaign trail. The election, after all, was only two months away.

That provided Leary with a sort of deadline.

The thought of that word—*dead*line—made Leary smile wider; he loved irony—it almost made life worth living.

In addition, Leary had also taped, or tacked up, hand-scrawled notes he'd taken—based upon newspaper and magazine accounts—on the President's habits and patterns.

But the man who was President at the moment was only part of Leary's display. Pictures clipped from books and magazines—he'd certainly be in trouble if several public libraries ever got hold of him!—gave this bedroom panorama a historical context.

Because next to the photos of the current Chief Executive were those of previous Presidents

Abraham Lincoln, James A. Garfield, William McKinley and John F. Kennedy.

There was, however, a difference: these pictures depicted moments of assassination—an archaic whorled illustration of Lincoln keeled over in his seat in his theater box at Ford Theater, behind him the smoking-pistol-in-hand of his dashing assassin; a similar ancient illustration of James A. Garfield, in the process of being shot in the back by a revolver-wielding assassin; another of William McKinley staggering backward in his reception line as a crazed-looking gunman fires a revolver; and, finally, jarringly modern in this context, a photograph—of John Kennedy slumped in his limo in Dallas as an agent ran toward him from the follow-up car, where other stunned agents rode the running boards.

Not all of the murder pictures were Presidential, but they depicted famous fallen political luminaries: a stunned, fatally wounded Anton Cermak, mayor of Chicago, being led away at a Miami rally for intended victim President-elect Franklin Delano Roosevelt; Robert Kennedy on his back in the kitchen of the Ambassador Hotel, looking skyward with the dazed look of the dead; Martin Luther King, Jr., down on the balcony floor of a Memphis motel.

Other faces, some of them smiling back at Leary, were taped to the wall: glowering, handsome, mustached John Wilkes Booth; preacherlike, bearded Charles J. Guiteau, fabled "disappointed office-seeker" who slew President Garfield; blond, cow-eyed anarchist Leon Czolgosz, who struck McKinley down; wild-eyed, wild-haired Sicilian Giuseppe Zangara, who shot Cermak; Zangara's twin, the dead-eyed Arab Sirhan Sirhan; that nondescript, face-in-the-crowd cracker, James Earl Ray . . .

And, of course, sullen, confused-looking, five o'clock–shadowed Lee Harvey Oswald, as well as such minor luminaries as George Wallace's attacker Arthur Bremer and Reagan's would-be killer, pasty, star-struck John Hinkley. Perhaps the latter didn't belong in this honor roll, thought Leary, frowning momentarily.

He had consciously omitted that mob hitman Jack Ruby, of course, and there was no way he would have ever included, in this gallery, John Lennon's assassin. That son of a bitch! Killing one of the Beatles! The *Beatles*! Leary would have gladly pulled the electric-chair switch on *that* asshole.

Humming "With a Little Help from My Friends," Leary gave his display one more touch. Returning his attention to the current President, he picked a picture he had taken himself, of the Prez waving, smiling at the People, and, with a deft, almost artistic flourish, the custodian of this museum traced an image in red felt-tip pen over the President's heart.

Leary grinned again. The perfect touch, he thought. The red image looked as if it belonged there—as if it were a printed part of the picture. Someday, no doubt, it *would* be printed in a book, this photograph he'd taken and the artful addition he'd made to it.

The cross hairs of a sniperscope.

2

Horrigan, leaning against a building in a black commercial district, ignoring occasional sullen looks from the funky folks who walked by, tapped his foot, but not to anybody's boom box, or to any inner music, either. His new partner was late. With what they had to do this morning, with the people they were dealing with, punctuality was a must.

He was checking his watch for the umpteenth time when the copper-brown Jeep Cherokee squealed up to the street corner.

Horrigan hopped quickly inside and his partner began apologizing immediately.

"Sorry I'm late," Al D'Andrea said. The dark-haired young agent—and he *was* young, still in his twenties—was earnest, blandly handsome, the Yuppie-ish sort that Horrigan had been enduring for much too long, now. Like Horrigan, D'Andrea was dressed in casual but expensive attire—a Ralph Lauren Polo shirt under a linen sport coat. Part of their undercover I.D. Very "Miami Vice."

"Just drive," Horrigan said.

D'Andrea drove. He didn't speak again until they were near the shipyards, approaching the marina on Chesapeake Bay.

"See, Ricky was upset," D'Andrea said. He was almost whining.

"Ricky? Who the fuck is Ricky?"

D'Andrea winced. "Ricky's my kid. He's only six years old, and it was his first day at this new school."

"Oh."

"I told him he had to be brave. It's hard bein' the new kid, you know." He shook his head, watching the road. "Poor little guy was really upset."

Horrigan said nothing.

"And then my wife had to be to work early, and—"

"Look, Al," Horrigan said with quiet impatience. "You work with me, you're on time. In our business, late is dead. Catch me?"

D'Andrea nodded glumly, driving. "I catch you."

Horrigan dug a small black Colt .38 from a sport-coat pocket and handed it to D'Andrea, who tucked it nervously into his own coat pocket. The marina loomed ahead, a world of shimmering blue littered with rich people's toys—yachts of every size.

They drove to a solitary slip, where the only ship docked was a handsome, immense, white-trimmed red sailboat that might have been ideal for a pleasure cruise. But somehow Horrigan didn't figure its captain would be in the market for a charter.

The two undercover agents walked onto the springy wharf, a cool fall breeze riffling their linen jackets. Three men waited next to the bobbing boat; the leader—a darkly handsome, immaculately groomed Yuppie with a ready smile and his own pale pastel Ralph Lauren wardrobe—called out, "Frank! Good to see you!"

This was Paul Mendoza; he was flanked by two more crooks in preppie attire: a strongarm named Jimmy Hendrickson, a big, blond college linebacker type who must've flunked out a decade ago and Raul, a wiry young Hispanic with a pencil-line mustache.

"And how are you, my friend?" Mendoza asked Horrigan, offering him a hand to shake, which he did.

"Not bad."

"You're a little late. We were getting worried."

"Don't you know the story about Miles Davis?"

"Who?" Mendoza asked, squinting.

"The great jazz trumpet player. It's a helluva story. But if you're in a hurry . . ."

Mendoza put his hand on Horrigan's shoulder. Gently. "Friends always have time for friends. Please. Share your story."

Horrigan smiled. Folded his arms. "Well. If you insist. See, Miles Davis had a big concert in the city. He was riding in back with his manager when he told the limo driver to stop at a drugstore. Miles went in, came back five minutes later with some smokes. Then the limo driver moved on and Miles had him stop at a liquor store. Miles went in, five minutes later came out with a bottle of bourbon. The limo driver drove on, and pretty soon Miles told him to stop at a newsstand. Miles got out, looked over the magazines, five minutes later came back with the new issue of *Downbeat*. His manager said,

'Miles! You're gonna be late for the show!' And Miles said, 'Hey, man, I can't be late for the show—I *am* the show.'"

Horrigan smiled at his own joke while the other men just looked at him. The sound of the boat's sail flapping gently in the wind was the only punctuation.

Then Mendoza laughed uproariously and the other men—a slightly unsettled D'Andrea included—smiled and laughed politely.

"You're one of a kind, Frank!" Mendoza said. "One of a kind."

Horrigan shrugged. "Anyway, sorry we're late. Traffic was a bitch."

"Life is a bitch, my friend. Life is a *son* of a bitch!" Mendoza turned to D'Andrea. "Al—go along with Jimmy and Raul for a minute, would you? Want a private word with Frank."

"Sure," D'Andrea said.

Hendrickson made a move toward him, as if to pat him down, and D'Andrea smiled uneasily and carefully lifted the .38 by its barrel from his own sport-coat pocket, as a show of good faith.

Mendoza frowned at him. "We said no guns. Aren't we friends?"

D'Andrea swallowed and said, "It's Frank's. His gun. His idea."

This kid is all heart, Horrigan thought sardonically.

"Go on aboard," Mendoza said, waving them on disenchantedly.

They padded onto the boat via the tiny gangplank—first Raul, then D'Andrea, finally Hendrickson—and Mendoza looked at Horrigan with disappointment.

"A gun, Frank? Don't you trust me?"

"Washington's a tough town. You can get mugged if you're not careful."

Mendoza smiled one-sidedly. "Do I need to have *you* patted down, Frank?"

"I'm unarmed. But feel free . . ."

Mendoza thought about it.

"Don't you trust me?" Horrigan asked, mildly mocking.

"You're one of a kind, Frank. You really are."

"So where's your funny money, Paul? Just 'cause I showed up late doesn't mean I got all day."

Mendoza showed him onto the boat, where on the bridge he offered a crisp one-hundred-dollar bill to Horrigan, who removed a jeweler's eyepiece from his pocket to examine the queer money's craftsmanship.

"Benjamin Franklin never looked better," Horrigan said.

He removed the eyepiece, dropped it in his pocket, then felt the texture of the phony bill with the thumbs and middle fingers of both hands.

"Paul," he said with an easy grin, "I think we're in business."

Mendoza took the bill from Horrigan's hands, and gazed at his "friend" with doleful eyes.

"Well, that's good news. But there's a problem, Frank."

"What kind of problem, Paul?"

He made a clicking in his cheek. "The worst kind."

With a curled finger, the counterfeiter motioned Horrigan to follow him, which the agent did, down into the lush living quarters below deck. They walked through the living room area, with its plush carpet, sofas with oversize pillows, and mirrored wet bar.

"Your friend Al . . . he kept asking questions about my label artist."

That was the time-honored term for a master of the counterfeiter's craft: the artisan who actually created the plates.

"Al's young," Horrigan said matter of factly. "He's curious. Learning."

Mendoza stopped, held up a single finger. "Too curious. Learning too much."

"Paul, he was vouched for . . ."

Mendoza sniffed the air. "You know what my nose tells me? Something smells. Something smells like the Secret Fucking Service."

"You gotta be wrong, pal—"

Mendoza's affable expression disappeared; a scowl, the likes of which chilled even a hardened agent like Horrigan, took its place.

"No. I had my boy Hendrickson follow your friend. He lives in Virginia, your friend."

"A lot of people live in—"

"His neighbors like him. He works for the government, they say."

"No shit," Horrigan said.

"No shit," Mendoza said, and opened the door to the galley, where D'Andrea sat, bound with rope into a chair, gagged with a bandanna, his eyes wide and filled with terror. Hendrickson was standing nearby with D'Andrea's gun in hand. Raul was watching from the sidelines, standing near a refrigerator, which was humming. Raul was humming a little himself, drinking milk from a carton, mixing his own thin mustache with a milk one.

Mendoza shrugged and lifted his hands, palms up. He put on a face of consternation. "How do I solve a problem like this, Frank?"

"Weight him down."

"What?"

"Otherwise the body might wash up on shore. Or just get puffy and bloat up and float up on the surface where some fisherman might spot him."

That made Mendoza smile; milk-mustached Raul laughed. D'Andrea seemed to be considering whether to pass out or just die.

"One of a kind, you are." Mendoza reached in his pocket and held out a small, ivory-handled automatic to Horrigan.

Horrigan didn't take it; just looked at it. "A gift, Paul? What's the occasion?"

Mendoza shook his head. "No occasion, Frank. More like—an obligation."

"Oh."

"I want *you* to pop him, Frank." Mendoza pointed his finger in the air and jerked his hand, as if firing, saying, "Pop!"

Horrigan kept an impassive gaze going. D'Andrea, however, was sweating, his eyes flashing with fear. Kid didn't have much experience. Horrigan did.

"See," Mendoza said, placing a friendly hand on the agent's shoulder, "I'm afraid maybe you're with him. That you're not *my* friend, that you're *his* friend."

"I'm everybody's friend—I'm a businessman."

Mendoza shrugged again. "So pop him and let's do some business."

Horrigan sighed. Looked at D'Andrea, face running with sweat, eyes filled with tears.

"I don't normally do this kind of thing," Horrigan said. "I'm just a businessman, like I said—but . . ."

He held his hand out and, reluctantly, accepted the gun from Mendoza. He hefted the little automatic. It felt light. He repressed a smile.

Hendrickson was training D'Andrea's .38 on the approaching Horrigan; under the sport coat was the strap of a shoulder holster. Raul was slouched against a counter, gulping at the carton occasionally, a tickled grin under his milky mustache. Raul had a revolver in his waistband.

Horrigan walked to the seated, bound D'Andrea, whose terror-filled eyes searched the agent's face for some message; but Horrigan knew better than to send one.

He placed the barrel of the automatic to his partner's temple; D'Andrea seemed to be trying to eat the gag, as he sucked vainly for air, his eyes— mercifully—squeezing shut, a few tears trickling down his cheeks. . . .

Horrigan squeezed the trigger.

Klik!

No bullet—but then Horrigan had figured that. Of course, poor D'Andrea had probably vacated both bowels and bladder by now. It would take a strong man not to.

"Bravo!" Mendoza said, taking the little gun from Horrigan's hand, slapping him on the back. "Bravo. And my apologies . . . I just had to find out, my friend."

Mendoza nodded at Hendrickson, who moved toward D'Andrea.

Then the counterfeiter slipped an arm around Horrigan's shoulder and said, "You like omelets,

Frank? I do. And I know just the best place for them. . . . They make a chili and cheese omelet to *die* for. . . ."

Mendoza started out, but Horrigan lagged.

Hendrickson, the revolver tucked in his waist now, was yanking a plastic bag down over D'Andrea's head. Raul, drinking his milk from the carton, watched with near boredom.

Mendoza's voice was mildly regretful. "You can't make omelets, Frank, without breaking a few eggs. . . . Come along, my friend."

Under the plastic bag, which was steaming up with his frantic breath, D'Andrea's eyes were bugged, his face turning blue; futilely, he wiggled and squirmed, but the big blond bad guy was holding the bag on tight, the plastic bunched in his fist, held at the back of D'Andrea's head.

"Maybe I want to watch," Horrigan said.

"Really?" Mendoza said from the galley doorway, interested, amused.

"This guy almost got *me* killed," Horrigan said. He moved closer, bending over, smiling, as if enjoying D'Andrea's bug-eyed torment. "How does a Secret Service asshole die, anyway?"

Hendrickson responded by smiling back at the bent-over Horrigan, a proud craftsman. And a dumb ass.

As if plucking a flower, Horrigan removed the revolver from the big blond's waist and shot him in the stomach.

The sound of the shot echoing in the small room, Horrigan whirled toward Raul, who with his free hand was going for the gun in his waistband; in the other hand was the milk carton, which took a bullet and spouted milk like blood, but Raul also took a bullet, and he just plain spouted blood.

And fell.

Horrigan heard another *klik* behind him, and turned and smiled as he saw Mendoza trying to shoot the little pearl-handled automatic.

"D'you forget, friend?" Horrigan asked him.

Mendoza swallowed thickly; he seemed very nervous now. Horrigan's hate-filled gaze was burning into him.

"No bullets, Paul," Horrigan said, moving to D'Andrea and yanking off the plastic bag, which once Hendrickson went down had ceased to be tight enough to suffocate him, but D'Andrea seemed nonetheless grateful to grab some real air. Even if it was the cordite-scorched air in this cramped cabin.

Mendoza had instinctively put his hands up. "Don't do it, man—don't do it!"

Horrigan was moving toward him, and Mendoza backed up until the counter stopped him. The dead bodies of his two flunkies were littering the galley floor; blood ran into milk, making a red-and-white marble design.

Horrigan smiled and placed the gun at Mendoza's temple.

Mendoza closed his eyes and his lips mouthed a prayer.

"I *am* the show, you son of a bitch," Horrigan said.

The front of Mendoza's pants were wet.

"By the way, asshole," Horrigan said, "you're under arrest."

3

∙∙∙∙∙∙∙∙∙∙∙∙∙∙∙∙∙∙∙∙∙∙∙∙∙∙∙∙∙∙

Late afternoon found Horrigan and his new partner, a still relieved but definitely frazzled Al D'Andrea, sitting in Horrigan's favorite neighborhood bar. Specifically, Horrigan was sitting at the piano, as usual. This time, he was playing, in tribute to their nautical ordeal, a chord-heavy jazz version of "La Mer," or as Bobby Darin used to put it, "Beyond the Sea." D'Andrea had pulled a stool up alongside the piano.

"You're telling me," D'Andrea was saying, "that you *knew* from the *weight* of the gun that it was empty?"

"Empty clip, yeah," Horrigan said, putting a little bounce into his piano playing.

"But couldn't there have been a slug in the fuckin' chamber?"

Keeping his left hand going, Horrigan reached for his glass of Jameson, sipped at it. "Never thought of that."

D'Andrea looked at his partner with eyes as wide

as when he'd been bound and gagged in the chair. Horrigan smiled blandly at him and started back in with the right hand. D'Andrea gulped at his drink, rolling eyes that were still bright with fear, shaking his head.

"The way you dropped those guys . . ." D'Andrea shivered. "That was cold, man."

"There's no warm way to do it."

"You . . . you killed guys before, Frank—haven't you?"

Horrigan nodded, shifted into a generic blues-jazz that was sort of "Stormy Monday," and sort of not.

D'Andrea leaned in, as if he were requesting a tune. "Doesn't it . . . get to you?"

"What?"

"Christ! Killing people."

"It would," Horrigan said, "if I let it."

Sitting back, D'Andrea gazed into his drink; stared into it, as if searching for the answers he was unlikely to get from his partner.

Then he said, quietly, suddenly, "I don't know if I'm cut out for this."

"Why?"

"Man . . . I was so fucking scared. . . ."

"Al—there's no other way to be than fucking scared when a fucking plastic bag is pulled over your fucking head."

D'Andrea laughed at the onslaught of obscenities. "Fucking A," he said.

Horrigan granted his partner a tiny smile, kept working the blues, walking the bass with his left hand.

Distracted, D'Andrea was staring at the TV high above the bar; on the screen, the President was speaking in the Rose Garden. Agents—all of whom Horrigan recognized—flanked the Man.

"Maybe," D'Andrea mused, hypnotized by the screen, "maybe if I worked Protection . . . I mean, who the hell needs this undercover shit?"

Horrigan grunted. "The idea of jumping in front of a gun appeals to you, Al? Where your biggest hope is that you can stop a bullet for the guy you're protecting?"

D'Andrea was looking into his drink again. "Maybe I don't have the . . . *nerve* for this line of work."

Horrigan stopped playing. He looked at his partner, hard, catching his eyes. "You're a good man. You'll make a good agent."

D'Andrea smirked. "How can you say that? After I blurted out that you gave me the gun, back there at the damn boat."

"It made sense saying that. Worked out fine."

"I don't know. I feel like I panicked."

"Trust me. You're gonna be fine. You're gonna do fine."

D'Andrea's response sounded damn near irritated. "How would you know? This is the longest conversation we ever had!"

Horrigan shrugged; he started playing again, back to the blues. "I know things about people. That's what they pay me for."

D'Andrea smiled; it seemed almost affectionate. He sat, finishing his drink—his one drink, he was driving—and listened to Horrigan play the blues. After a while, the senior agent checked his watch.

"You wanna get somethin' to eat?" Horrigan asked.

"What?" D'Andrea smirked. "Don't tell me you know this great place for omelets!"

"I was thinking more along the lines of Italian. Honor of my new partner."

D'Andrea climbed off his stool. "No thanks. I got something I have to do."

"Such as?"

"Go home and kiss my wife and hug my kid."

"Not a bad plan at that."

D'Andrea extended his hand. "Thanks, partner—for saving my life."

"Hey—like Mendoza said, I'm one of a kind."

They shook hands; the gesture had a certain warmth that touched Horrigan, though he wouldn't have admitted it for anything short of a Miles Davis boxed CD set.

"One-of-a-kind Horrigan," D'Andrea said. "That's what I been hearin', ever since I got into this town. A lot of guys warned me about you."

"Warned you what?"

D'Andrea grinned. "Warned me Horrible Horrigan was one colossal pain in the ass."

"Nice of 'em. Accurate, too." He patted the younger agent on the arm. "See you at the office, kid."

D'Andrea's eyes widened. "Oh, shit—the office!" He dug in his sport-coat pocket and came back with a slip of paper. "Completely the hell forgot! When we checked in at the office, after that marina madness, Monroe had an assignment for us!"

"An assignment? Where the hell was I?"

"Getting debriefed. It's not really an assignment, Frank—just another wacko we're supposed to check out. . . . Maybe it can wait till tomorrow."

"Better do it today."

"You're probably right. . . . Damn. Give me a second to call home—"

Horrigan snatched the slip of paper out of his partner's hand. "Just *go* home."

"What about the wacko?"

"Consider it done."

"I'll be glad to come along. . . ."

"Kiss the wife. Hug the kid. Go."

The fear was finally out of D'Andrea's eyes. "Thanks, partner," he said.

After D'Andrea had gone, Horrigan finished his Jameson and glanced at the address.

"Nice neighborhood," he said sarcastically, to no one.

The landlady leading Horrigan down the darkened hallway of the decrepit apartment building had an accent, but the agent wasn't sure what. Lithuanian, maybe? At any rate, she was fat and as homely as the hairy mole on her cheek—not the sort of company Horrigan might have hoped for this evening.

"I don't snoop, mister," she was saying, trundling ahead of him, "I am not no nosey landlady. But the smoke alarm, it was going off."

"You did the right thing," Horrigan said in his best Jack Webb monotone.

"I hear that thing goin' off, I get scared. But not so scared as when I see what there is *inside*. . . ."

She stopped at a door marked 314, knocked. Horrigan's eyelids were heavy. It had been a long day; it was turning into a pointlessly long night.

The fat landlady was still yakking: "The smoke, it was just from crumbs in the oven that got left on."

She knocked again. Still no answer.

"Should I unlock the door, mister?"

"I can't ask you to do that," he said. "I don't have a warrant. On the other hand, you're the landlady. If you want to go in, and would like to have me for company, that's your decision."

She nodded vigorously. "That's what I want! That's what I want, all right."

And she unlocked the door with her passkey.

She waddled her way through a small, dark entryway, guiding him through a cheaply, sparsely furnished kitchen where the cracked plaster walls were smoke-stained and the smell of those burnt crumbs hung like a dirty curtain that refused brushing aside. At the end of the hall, she hit a light switch and stepped to one side, pointing toward an open doorway. Her eyes were childish and wide, a schoolkid tattling.

Horrigan entered the small cell of a bedroom, where dreary wallpaper so faded its pattern couldn't be discerned was peeling away; but one of those walls was decorated with clipped photos and magazine illustrations and eight-by-ten glossies. Horrigan's sister, many years ago, had decorated her bedroom walls like this, with images of Fabian, Frankie Avalon and Bobby Rydell.

But the person who had erected this shrine did not have teen idols in mind.

This person worshiped at the altar of Lee Harvey Oswald and Sirhan Sirhan. This person slept in a single, cotlike bed from which the images of slain Presidents could be lovingly studied. This person had penned, in a hand both clear and clearly disturbed, details of the current President's habit patterns.

This person had drawn, on a photo, in red, a

sniperscope target on the chest of the President of the United States.

"Thirty-one years I am in this country," the landlady was saying. "I love this country—these United States. I have visited the White House five, six times. Me—myself—personally! Only in the United States can just anybody go to the house of the President and visit. . . ."

On a scuffed-up secondhand dresser sat a row of books; their subject was uniform: assassins and assassinations, leaning on JFK conspiracy tomes.

"So when I see this . . . these killing things," she continued, "I call police. . . . They say, call Secret Service. I did, but you don't come for two days!"

Horrigan, not touching anything, knelt to look at a stack of videotapes, all of which pertained to the Kennedy assassination.

"Ma'am," he said, "the President gets over fourteen hundred death threats a year. We have to check every single one. That takes time."

"Well, I'm glad you come, even if you *are* late," she said.

He didn't have the energy to tell her the Miles Davis story, to explain that he *was* the show.

"You said the tenant's name is McCrawley?"

"Joseph McCrawley," she said, nodding forcefully. "From Colorado Denver!"

On a small dresser were two items of interest. One of them was a sleek, futuristic model car, plastic. It sat on a stack of hobby magazines devoted to model collecting.

The other item of interest was a handwritten sheet of paper which said: "THEY CAN GAS ME, BUT I AM FAMOUS. I HAVE ACHIEVED IN ONE DAY

WHAT IT TOOK ROBERT KENNEDY ALL HIS LIFE TO DO."

Horrigan recognized the quote, but even if he hadn't, guessing the author's name—Sirhan Sirhan—wouldn't have been much of a trick.

He had a closer look at the photos on the wall; seeing Robert Kennedy lying on the floor, after the shooting, made Horrigan's stomach knot up. Bobby. Feisty little bastard. Even after all these years, Horrigan still missed him. . . .

His gaze traveled to another photo: Bobby's brother John, slumped in his limo on that bloody street in Dallas. An agent ran toward the President from the follow-up car, where three other agents stood on running boards.

"I still remember like yesterday," the woman was saying. "I cry and cry. . . ."

Horrigan remembered, too.

He was in the photo.

Across the street from the apartment building in this rundown neighborhood—due for destruction in coming urban renewal—a man of medium height stood in the shadows looking up at the third floor, where behind a drawn shade, shapes moved.

Mitch Leary frowned at the sight, at the *thought*, of someone in his apartment. He would have to move on, now. Damn!

Then the shade was raised, and one of the shapes became a man, standing in the window of Leary's room, looking down on the city street.

Face tight with irritation, Leary lifted his small pair of high-powered binoculars and focused them in on the face of the intruder in his apartment.

Suddenly the skull-mask of Leary's face was grinning.

"Frank Horrigan!" he whispered to the street. Juices were racing in him. What a wonderful irony!

"Delicious," Leary said, and tucked his binoculars in his raincoat pocket, and waited.

4

Joseph McCrawley of "Colorado Denver" (as the landlady had put it) had been dead since 1961.

Or so Jack Okura, at the Intelligence Division Office, said—and his computers never lied. McCrawley, it seemed, had died at age eleven. The man using this long-dead child's name, the man whose bedroom was a sick shrine to assassination, had undoubtedly manipulated the system into giving him a duplicate of the McCrawley birth certificate, in order to get a driver's license and build a false identity.

So, the next afternoon, Horrigan—with both his partner Al D'Andrea and a warrant in tow—returned to the rundown apartment house and stood in the hallway before room 314 and rapped his fist on the door.

"Federal agents," he barked. "Open the door!"

Though the heavyset landlady had declared herself "no snoop," she watched from the end of the wall, craning her fat neck. Her eyes became saucers as Horrigan and D'Andrea drew their revolvers from holsters beneath the shoulders of crisp business suits.

D'Andrea waved the woman back, as Horrigan used the passkey she had given them to unlock the door.

The older agent stood to one side, back to the wall, and the younger agent stood to the other side, likewise, guns in hand, barrels up. Horrigan reached his left hand over and around to turn the knob; then, with the side of his left foot, kicked open the door.

After the sharp sound of the kick, and the door slamming into the wall, there was only silence.

D'Andrea, clearly nervous, looked at Horrigan, whose shrug was barely perceptible. The senior agent went in first, slowly, carefully, moving through the empty kitchen, where the scorched smell still hung. No sign of anybody. No sounds but their own light, cautious footsteps.

Horrigan positioned himself with back to the wall again, beside the open doorway of the bedroom.

Then with a sudden movement, he filled the doorway in a crouch, fanning the revolver around the room.

Which was completely empty.

Empty, that is, but for the cheap furnishings, the drawers of the bureau and small dresser yawning open, also empty. The single bed was neatly made, boot-camp style. The assassination books and tapes, the sleek model car and the hobby magazines, all were gone. And the wallpapered walls had been stripped of their grotesque pinups—with one exception.

Holstering his revolver, Horrigan walked slowly

toward the sole remaining photo.

D'Andrea was right behind him. "Jesus," he breathed.

It was the Dallas photo, of course, the slumped President in the limo, an agent running toward him, three other agents riding the running board of the follow-up car.

The head of the nearest of those follow-up car agents was circled in red, reminding Horrigan of the photo he'd seen in this room last night, a photo with a red target traced on the current President's chest.

"Why, that's you," D'Andrea said. His voice was hushed, stunned. "Jesus, Frank—you were right."

"What do you mean?"

"You *are* the show."

That evening, after a long day of canvassing the other tenants in the building and going over the now-vacant apartment with lab technicians, Horrigan was getting a ride home from D'Andrea in the latter's late-model Pontiac Sunbird. Horrigan didn't own a car—he used public transportation and bummed rides.

Staring out the rider's window into the night and the city it shrouded, Horrigan wanted to brood, not talk. But his silence apparently made D'Andrea anxious. The younger agent seemed determined to make conversation.

"Not one goddamn print. Can you imagine?"

Horrigan said nothing. He knew a usable finger-print was harder to find than the right woman, but he said nothing.

"Brady said the guy must be good."

Brady was the tech who had used a fancy-ass Omniprint 1000 laser on the apartment, to no avail.

"I wouldn't describe him that way," Horrigan muttered.

"What way?"

"'Good.'"

D'Andrea nodded, watched the road. The hum of tires and traffic noise lulled Horrigan; he closed his eyes. He wanted sleep to come. He was even willing to risk the dream for it.

"Man, this guy sure fits the profile," D'Andrea said.

"Bullshit."

"Huh?"

"The profile's bullshit." Horrigan sat up. "You can't predict who's going to be an assassin."

D'Andrea frowned. "Well . . . he's a loner, right? He was studying past assassinations, wasn't he?"

"So are most of the high-school students in this country."

"Frank, back at Brunswick, in one of the first training sessions, they said—"

"I don't give a fuck what they said."

"Jeez! Retaining water, are we?"

Now D'Andrea brooded, and Horrigan couldn't get comfortable in the car seat.

Finally Horrigan exploded. "You think I screwed up or something?"

D'Andrea, surprised, looked over wide-eyed, saying, "Huh?"

"You think I should've waited around for the guy last night—don't you?"

"I didn't say that, Frank."

"Jesus! I wish I'd had *you* with me, Al, with your vast experience and all."

"Frank . . ."

"Now I got to be satisfied with your twenty-twenty fucking hindsight."

"Hey, I didn't say *anything*. . . ."

Horrigan rubbed his eyes. "We keep files on over forty-seven thousand assholes who at one time or another've threatened the Big Chief. Not *one* of 'em has ever tried to kill a President. Not one!"

"Frank . . ."

"Hell, by those odds, just by opening a file on the son of a bitch, I eliminated him."

They rode in silence for a while. Horrigan's face was hot; he felt awkward, embarrassed. As they were nearing his apartment, he pointed to the bar on K Street and said softly, "There's a parking place. Pull up and I'll buy you a drink."

D'Andrea pulled over, but said, uneasily, "I got to get home, Frank."

"To the wife and kid."

"Right."

"What's her name? The little woman."

"Ariana."

The poetry of it stopped Horrigan; he ran the name around in his mind for a few moments. Then he said, "Pretty name."

"Pretty woman."

He touched his partner's forearm. "Lucky guy."

D'Andrea let him off, and Horrigan headed for the bar, then suddenly changed his mind. It had been the kind of day that could send him reeling seriously off the wagon.

So he said, "Fuck it," and just walked home.

Distracted, the image of that Dallas photo with his face circled in red burning in his brain, Horrigan shuffled into his messy apartment, slipping out of his suit coat, climbing out of his shoulder holster. He removed his handcuffs and extendible baton from his belt, threw them on the coffee table, where they joined some bullets and CD jewel boxes. Untying his tie, yanking it free, he stretched his neck, a man free of a noose.

He allowed himself two inches of Jameson, and pushed on the CD player—"Kind of Blue" was still in the machine—and flopped into the easy chair that faced the stereo, allowing the purifying sounds of Miles Davis to wash over him.

He had almost nodded off when the phone on the table beside him gave off its shrill ring. Using his remote to turn down the stereo, he spoke into the phone: "Yeah?"

"Frank Horrigan?"

The voice was soft. Excited, but not nervous. A man, but not masculine.

"Yeah?" Horrigan said again, sitting up a little.

"The Secret Service agent?"

Horrigan frowned. "Yeah—if this is Publisher's Clearinghouse, you know where to send the check."

"My God!" The excitement in the voice was like a child's. "I can't believe it's really *you*. . . ."

Hairs stood like needles on the back of Horrigan's neck. "Who the hell *is* this?"

After a long pause, the almost childishly breathless voice returned: "That *was* you, in my apartment last night—wasn't it?"

Horrigan swallowed. "McCrawley?"

"That name isn't useful anymore."

"Surely you have another."

"How about . . . Booth."

As in John Wilkes.

"Why not Oswald?" Horrigan suggested acidly.

The sarcasm seemed lost on the caller, who mused, "I don't believe he acted alone. What do *you* think, Frank? What's the insider's opinion?"

"Where are you?"

"Close by. Did you go back to my place, Frank? Did you see the message I left you?"

"I saw it," Horrigan said. He rose, stretching the phone cord to the window, where he looked out on what seemed to be a deserted street. He glanced at his watch: approaching midnight. "You did one hell of a cleanup job. The techs were impressed—only found one fingerprint."

Unfazed, the voice seemed almost amused. "If they found a print, it was yours, not mine."

"Listen . . . my apartment's kind of a mess. I could use a good housekeeper. Would you consider coming in?"

"I don't do windows, Frank." Still amused.

"What *do* you do?"

Another long pause, broken up only by Booth's heavy breathing, obscene caller–style.

Then the almost effeminate voice said: "This is very exciting, Frank—isn't it? I feel I know you."

"You do, huh?"

"I've read all about you . . . seen so many photos. You were JFK's favorite agent, weren't you?"

Horrigan winced. *You fucker,* he thought.

"I was just another agent," he said.

"Don't bullshit me! You used to play touch football on the White House lawn with Jack and Bobby and the whole gang. Singing Irish folk songs on Air Force One. Boating at Hyannis Port. You know what you were, Frank?"

"Why don't you tell me, Booth."

"You were the best and the brightest, Frank."

Horrigan's jaw tightened.

"But you know what?" the voice continued. "That was a long, long time ago. Are you still good, Frank?"

"Try me."

"What do you think I'm doing, Frank? Tell me— what's kept you in the game all these years?"

Horrigan's hand gripped the phone; it was like a part of his fist. But he kept his voice casual. "Why don't we get together for a drink? There's a bar near here. I'll tell you my life story."

"I *know* your life story. And as much as I'd love to get together, I think the less you know about me, the better."

"Why's that, Booth?"

"Because," the voice said coyly.

"Because why?"

"Because I'm planning to kill the President."

Horrigan's heart was racing, but he kept his voice calm. "Aw, now, Booth . . . you shouldn't've said that. You know, threatening the President's life is a federal offense. You can go to jail even if you're just kidding around."

The coy voice was suddenly a cutting knife: "Do you think I'm kidding around, Frank?"

The words, and the way they were spoken, chilled Horrigan.

"What have you got against the big guy, anyway, Booth?"

"Remember that Beatles song, Frank?"

"What Beatles song?"

" 'With a Little Help from My Friends.' "

"You gonna have some help, Booth?"

The caller's laugh was oddly gentle, like rippling water. "Frank, Frank . . . it's just a song. I'm not planting clues. You're going to have to find your *own* clues . . . if you can."

"Let me ask you something, Booth."

"Please, Frank."

"Are you willing to trade your life for the President's? 'Cause that, pal, is what it's going to take."

It took the caller a moment to reply; it was as if he were thinking through the exact phrasing he wished to use.

He said, "John F. Kennedy said that all someone needs is a willingness to trade his life for the President's—right?"

"Right."

"Well . . ."

"Well what, Booth?"

"Well, I'm willing."

The faint sound of a fire engine leached over the wire.

"You know, Frank, I just can't get over the delicious irony."

Seething, Horrigan said, "What delicious irony?"

"You being intimately involved with the assassinations of two presidents."

The fire-engine siren was outside Horrigan's own window, now! He looked out and saw the clanging red vehicle blaze through the intersection. Booth *was* close by!

"Hang on a second, pal," Horrigan said easily, "I got something on the stove that's boiling over. . . . I'll be right back—"

And he tossed the phone gently on the sofa and ran like a madman out of the apartment, grabbing his revolver from his shoulder holster on the table as he went.

He tore down the stairs, damn near knocking over the couple next door, who were coming up, arm in arm. He was on the street within seconds, and ran toward the corner where he'd seen the fire truck whiz by. Summoning speed he didn't know he still possessed, Horrigan sprinted around the corner and almost ran smack into a phone booth.

Where an abandoned receiver dangled on its cord, spinning.

His breath was coming hard now; heart pounding, his age catching up with him. Revolver in hand, at the ready, he looked in every direction, taking a few steps this way, and that, like a man who couldn't make up his mind which way to go; his eyes desperately searched the intersecting streets.

Nobody. Nothing.

Not even the sound of a vehicle screeching away.

A couple of bars were open that Booth might have ducked into, and Horrigan would check them out, but what good would it do?

Who the hell was he looking for, anyway?

5

The White House glistened in the sun, a perfect symbol of the Presidency, its vast lawn immaculate and impossibly green even in the fall. The living quarters and public rooms, viewed by tourists and such local citizens as the fat Lithuanian landlady Horrigan had encountered, were in the familiar plantationlike Mansion; the White House working offices, including the Oval Office, were in the less familiar West Wing.

And across the street, specifically across closed-off West Executive Avenue, was the baroque monstrosity known as the Old Executive Office Building. This massive rust-colored granite edifice, with its many pillars and windows, rose like a many-tiered, out-of-control wedding cake; considered for years an eyesore, the controversy over the O.E.O.B. had been decided by President Kennedy, who decreed its complete renovation.

Perhaps because of the Kennedy connection, Horrigan had an unnatural affection for this grotesque building, from the top of which he could easily imagine the Addams Family tilting a cauldron of hot oil onto unwelcome visitors. It was here that the Presidential Protective Division of the United States Secret Service kept its command center.

Horrigan and D'Andrea's footsteps echoed down a vast corridor. Their photographic I.D. badges were clipped to their suit coats. D'Andrea had his field notebook in hand and was reading from a page headed "Booth."

"It's weird," he said. "All the tenants noticed him . . . you know, passed him on the stairs and so on . . . but nobody really *saw* the guy."

"Typical," Horrigan said.

"Depending on who you talk to, our man is either five-eight, or six-two . . . weighs in at 165, or maybe 180. . . ."

"And his age," Horrigan said with mild disgust, "is somewhere between twenty-eight and forty-five."

D'Andrea nodded, sighed and slapped his notebook shut.

They were standing before the door marked with the Secret Service/Treasury Department insignia and the words "PRESIDENTIAL PROTECTIVE DIVISION." The room they entered—the Bullpen—was an expansive desk-cluttered area buzzing with special agents and clerical workers; one wall was covered with charts listing detail assignments as well as the movements of the division's designated protectees: the President, Vice President and various federal officials.

Beyond a wall of windows loomed a view of the West Wing of the White House. To one side of the room, in a glass-enclosed booth, on the screens of a bank of twenty-five monitors, exterior and interior views of the White House were constantly being viewed by a pair of agents.

Horrigan and his partner moved through the Bullpen and through an open door into the large, stately office of Sam Campagna, Assistant Director in Charge of Protection. Campagna was one of the two or three most powerful officials in the Secret Service—even the deputy director had less influence.

Seated at the conference table, surrounded by photos of past Presidents and the Secret Service details that guarded them, were Campagna himself and three agents, two men and a woman.

Horrigan and D'Andrea waited for an opening in the conversation.

Bill Watts—a slender, dark-haired, arrogant bastard in his late thirties—was characteristically irritated.

He was saying, "White House Advance just canceled Miami and scheduled Albany and Boston instead."

"For when?" the female agent asked.

Horrigan didn't know her, but he wouldn't have minded: she was lanky, nicely constructed, her hair reddish-blond, worn up—she was as attractive and well composed as a network anchorwoman. She wore a cream-colored blouse under a well-tailored copper business suit.

"For tomorrow," Watts said bitterly.

The woman sighed.

Matt Wilder—an old friend of Horrigan's, in his early forties, an easygoing guy who knew how to go with the flow—was trying to calm the waters.

Matt shrugged and said, "The President's trailing

in the polls by twenty points in the northeast. His staff's panicked—can't blame 'em."

The woman arched an eyebrow and said, "When he was leading, they were panicked, too—'cause they didn't *trust* the polls."

Solid old Sam Campagna—his beefy frame overflowing his chair, white hair cut Marine short, flinty gray eyes taking everything in—had seen it all in his fifty-some years. He gave the realist's view—or was it the cynic's?

He said, "Two months before election, panic is what you get on a *good* day."

Watts smirked darkly. "We're going to have to pull agents in, from here to hell and back."

"Do it, then." Campagna smiled over at Horrigan and D'Andrea. "Frank, I'm glad to see you're still alive."

Horrigan said, "I'm glad you're glad, Director."

Campagna stood and ambled over like a trained bear to greet his old friend; they shook hands, and traded a glance that contained a world of memories.

"I hear you and your partner had some fun yesterday," Campagna said, referring to the Mendoza arrest at the marina.

"An outing, now and then," Horrigan said, "is good for the soul."

"You haven't come to see me in God knows how long."

"I'll come anytime I'm asked, Director."

The affable Campagna moved to D'Andrea, shook hands with him, saying, "So you're the new partner. How do you like working with a certified dinosaur?"

D'Andrea, apparently a little thrown by finding the brass so unpretentious, said, "It's a learning experience, all right, sir."

Campagna ushered the two agents to the table. "Frank," he said, "you know Matt Wilder, of course. . . ."

Matt had stood, and was grinning as he reached across the table to shake Horrigan's hand.

"I sure do," Horrigan said. "Still owes me twenty bucks from Super Bowl Twenty-One." As an aside, he told D'Andrea, "Son of a bitch insists on betting Denver."

"It's a dirty job," Matt said, "but somebody's gotta do it."

Campagna was gesturing to Watts, who didn't rise. "You know Bill Watts, I'm sure, the agent in charge—and this is Lilly Raines."

Horrigan nodded to Watts, saying, "Bill," and then smiled at Lilly Raines, saying, "It's amazing."

"What is?" she asked, smiling wryly as he shook her warm hand.

"How the secretaries around here just keep getting prettier and prettier."

She didn't miss a beat, and the smile just got wryer. "Like the field agents just keep getting older and older?"

Horrigan rewarded her comeback with a little grin.

"Ouch," Matt said.

Campagna didn't seem to know whether to be embarrassed or amused. "Lilly's an agent, Frank."

"I figured," he said. "Just wanted to see if she had a sense of humor."

"Did I pass?" she asked.

"Flying colors," he said.

Checking his watch, Campagna said, "Let's get started, shall we? We don't have all that much time."

Everyone found a seat at the conference table. Horrigan noticed Lilly looking past him with a brief, sudden look of surprise; he glanced behind him and saw a photo on the wall of a beaming John Kennedy and a detail of agents. One of them was Horrigan, a hundred years and a thousand wrinkles ago.

Campagna was looking at a report sheet, which he passed along to Watts. "So. Tell us about this guy. I guess we're calling him 'Booth' for the present. What's the deal on him?"

Horrigan said, flatly, "He's a definite lookout."

A "lookout" was Secret Service jargon for an extremely dangerous individual who had threatened the President. Of the 40,000 individuals and groups the Service considered to be potential hazards to the President, around 350—with a history of violence and/or mental illness—were so classified.

"You really think he's dangerous?" Matt asked.

"He is," Horrigan said.

Lilly frowned in thought. "You say that as if it's a fact."

"It is."

"How do you know that?"

"I just do." He smiled a little. "I know things about people. It's what they pay me for."

Watts was frowning, but not in thought; just plain frowning.

He asked, "Might I ask why you didn't take appropriate steps that first night? Then we might *know* something besides what your gut instincts tell you."

Prick.

Horrigan's smile was only technically a smile. "We had kind of a busy day, Bill."

"Too busy to investigate properly?"

"I was on my way home from killing a guy."

Lilly raised another eyebrow. Campagna seemed to be trying not to smile. Matt wasn't even trying.

Watts pressed on. "Your reports say that you were only in the apartment for, what? Ten minutes?"

"I didn't have a warrant."

"Given your . . . reputation in undercover work, I wouldn't think . . ."

"I guess you wouldn't."

"What?"

"Think." He looked at Campagna. "Am I paranoid, or is Bill, here, busting my balls?"

Lilly seemed amused, but also a little uneasy. "Both of the above?"

"I just think," Watts said, looking a little flustered, "that considering Agent Horrigan's reputation, he might have—"

"What reputation is that, Bill?" Horrigan asked.

Watts threw the report on the table. "Forget it."

"What's my reputation? You referred to it twice."

"Let's drop it."

Campagna said, "Let's get back on track, boys and girls. . . ."

"You know, Bill," Horrigan said, "I understand you. Once upon a time, I was *almost* as smug as you. . . ."

Watts stood, flushed. "I don't have time for this shit. I got seventy-five agents to pull out of Miami." He paused at the door to look back at Campagna and say, "Keep me posted, will you, Sam?"

Campagna nodded as Watts exited, then let loose

a sigh, shook his head. "What do we do about this guy?"

"Watts, you mean?" Horrigan said. "How about a transfer to the Omaha field office?"

"I meant Booth," Campagna said patiently.

Horrigan got serious; he glanced at D'Andrea, who was keeping quiet. "Al and me, we're checking what we can. . . . In the meantime, obviously, we need to put a tap on my phone."

Campagna nodded. "That makes sense. Anything else you think it'll take, just say the word."

Lilly's eyes narrowed. "You seem sure Booth'll call you again."

"Oh, he'll call again," Horrigan said. His mouth twitched. "We're pals."

Later that afternoon, in Ebbitt's Grill—a dark, smoky, polished-wood male bastion across from the Treasury Building—Horrigan sat at the bar, where he was allowing Sam Campagna to buy him a drink.

"What did Watts mean, Sam?" he asked, almost playful.

"What do you mean?"

"This reputation I'm supposed to have. What is it, exactly?"

"You know damn well."

He grinned; swirled his Jameson in its glass. "That I'm a borderline burnout with the people skills of a concentration camp commandant?"

Campagna summoned a smile for that, but it seemed weary.

Finally, swirling his own drink, bourbon, he said, "You know, Frank—if you were half as smart as we all used to think you were . . . you'd retire."

"I could've by now."

"Sure."

"But you know what I really want?"

"No low back pain and a woman under fifty?"

Horrigan grinned again. "Well, that, too."

"What?"

He sipped his Jameson. "To be assigned to the President."

Campagna damn near did a spit take. "The PPD? After all these years? Christ, a dinosaur like you . . ."

"You said I could have anything I wanted, to stop this guy. Well this is what I want."

"Why, in God's name?"

Horrigan gave his old friend the hardest gaze he had; and he had a few. "This motherfucker is going to make a try, Sam. It's not a bluff. It's for real. And I want to be there when he does."

Campagna stared at him blankly; a tic jumped in the Director's cheek.

"We all know," Horrigan said solemnly, "every agent knows, it's going to happen someday."

"What?"

"The moment of truth. I had one in Dallas, a long time ago . . . and I blew it."

"You didn't blow it. . . ."

"I fucking blew it. And I want something that few of us get: a second chance. When my moment of truth comes around the second time, I'm gonna be ready, Sam. Ready."

Campagna blew out a lot of air. Shook his head. Swirled his drink. Said, "Watts would fight me tooth and nail on this."

"Fuck him. You're the boss. Besides, you owe me thirty years' worth of favors."

Campagna was still shaking his head; now he rolled his eyes. "If you only knew how many times I covered your ass, and saved that damn job of yours. . . ."

"Give me this, Sam. I need this."

"What about the Booth investigation?"

"D'Andrea can cover it. I'll keep a hand in on the side. Shit, man—this *is* the goddamn Booth investigation!"

The Director stared into his drink, as if looking for a way out of this.

"You really want to stand post again, Frank? At your age?"

"I think I can find a pair of orthopedic shoes somewhere, Boss. Yeah."

"All right, you asshole."

"I love you, too."

Campagna's gray eyes narrowed. "By the way, Frank—Watts is nowhere near as smug as you were when you had Kennedy's ear."

Horrigan shrugged. "Nobody's perfect."

6

Two officers with the Secret Service Uniformed Division took their positions on a rooftop overlooking Massachusetts Avenue on this unseasonably warm autumn morning.

One, a sharpshooter in orange-lensed sunglasses, readied his high-powered rifle with sniperscope as casually as a professional golfer might heft his putter before an easy, but crucial, shot.

The other uniformed officer studied the approaching Presidential motorcade through his binoculars.

He watched them come slowly into view—five police motorcycles, two police squad cars, one unmarked police car, two Secret Service vehicles, the Presidential limousine, a black van, several press cars, two more squad cars and three more cops on motorcycles. It looked like a very big deal indeed.

The sharpshooter, soaked in sweat, smirked down at the caravan. "So what's he up to, today?"

The other officer lowered his binoculars and

smirked back. "Big doin's—he's takin' the President of France out for lunch."

"Do tell."

"Yeah—a Chinese joint on K Street."

Sweat trickled down the sides of the sharpshooter's nose from behind the sunglasses.

"God," he said. "Couldn't he've just ordered some damn carry-out for the frog prince?"

Sweating, panting, Horrigan walked quickly alongside the Presidential limo, one of half a dozen agents positioned on either side of the vehicle as it motored down the avenue to cheers from a sizable crowd, fists flapping tiny American and French flags. In the oversize windows of the parade limo, the presidents of the two countries were smiling and waving back at the enthusiastic throng.

Goddamn this hot day, Horrigan thought. *Just my fucking luck to catch a day like this, first time out.*

He squinted into the sunlight—he was the only agent not wearing sunglasses—and kept his eyes on the crowd as it blurred by him. The pace he was having to maintain reminded Horrigan how much a young man's game protective duty was.

Even a young man, in top physical condition, could be burned out by this work. Three years tops before you got rotated off this stress-inducing assignment. And he'd asked, begged, to be put back on!

Chatter in his earpiece notified Horrigan, like the other agents, of a sudden change in plan.

The limo came to an abrupt stop, and Horrigan and the others—among them Lilly Raines, in a loose tailored pants suit, blood-red blouse and flat shoes—formed a perimeter around the car as the two presidents emerged, wearing great big twin shit-eating grins, to "press the flesh" in the time-honored politician's way—shaking hands with what had turned out to be a surprisingly large and demonstrative crowd.

Two months before an election, trailing in some of the polls, the Chief Executive could hardly pass up this big-time media op.

All but glued to the President's right shoulder was Bill Watts; the senior agent on a detail like this made himself the Commander in Chief's Siamese twin.

Meanwhile, out in front of the two presidents, Horrigan was training his well-practiced stone-faced zombie stare on the crowd, intimidating them even as he scrutinized each face, catalogued every movement. When a scruffy homeless-looking character in an old Army jacket nudged his way to the front, Horrigan gave him the patented hard, impenetrable stare and the guy suddenly looked queasy and faded back into the crowd.

Glancing over at Lilly, Horrigan almost smiled, which would have taken the edge off the facade he was presenting; but Lilly's version of the "stare" was so forced it almost seemed comical. For the first time where she was concerned, he gave into his sexist proclivities and thought of her as a "girl."

But even so, he knew she'd get there. She'd get there.

Now he noticed that she was focused on a specific face in this crowd; he searched for it, found it: a Middle Eastern–looking man reaching into a canvas bag. His appearance wasn't suspicious—he wore a black business suit with no tie—but his manner seemed furtive. It wasn't racist, from a Secret

Service point of view, to look at a Middle Easterner and think of Holy Wars that might spill over onto the President.

Horrigan watched Lilly speak into her cuff-clipped mike and, within seconds, two agents in casual street dress moved along either side of the dark little guy. They braced him, one of them dipping a hand into the canvas bag, and coming back with—a camera.

Horrigan didn't register his relief; but he did note, to himself, and with some satisfaction, Lilly's quick, professional response.

Finally, the pair of presidents, waving to the cheering crowd, made their way back to the limo and got in, Watts closing the door behind them and climbing in front, next to the driver.

Now the limo was moving again, and that meant Horrigan had to get moving again, too. Huffing, puffing, wiping his clammy brow, he clipped along, keeping the pace. It wasn't easy. But he kept pace.

Watts, in the front-seat rider's window, looked out at Horrigan, and could obviously see the toll this duty was taking on the older agent. The prick smirked faintly, then turned to face forward.

Horrigan felt proud of himself—not so much for keeping up, as for resisting giving that smug little bastard the finger.

Binoculars focused on the motorcade, following the Presidential limousine like a magnet on metal. Then the gaze of the binoculars shifted, zoomed, centering in on Special Agent Horrigan, as he struggled along, sometimes almost stumbling, looking like he might faint any second.

"Poor baby. . . ."

The binoculars were lowered—not by a uniformed Secret Service officer atop a building, but by an observer from some distance away, at the rear of the crowd.

The observer smiled faintly.

"Poor baby," Mitch Leary said again, from the shadows of a building's recessed doorway.

Feet up on a chair, Horrigan was sleeping soundly, and not dreaming, when he felt hands on his chest; he opened his eyes and somebody was unbuttoning his shirt!

"What the fuck . . ."

It was a fresh-faced kid in white.

"Get the hell offa me!"

The kid, a paramedic, jumped back in wide-eyed shock, bumping into a second, slightly older paramedic.

Dead-tired Horrigan, who had dozed off in a soft chair in the lounge at one end of the Protective Division bullpen, now found himself staring at Sam Campagna, Matt Wilder, Lilly Raines and half a dozen other agents. Some of their faces seemed concerned, others were ripe with barely suppressed laughter.

The paramedic, embarrassed and a little shaken, said, "Jeez, I'm sorry, mister. . . ."

The older paramedic chimed in: "Yeah, we got a call there was a cardiac arrest case in here!"

Campagna, with concern that might have been real, leaned in to put a hand on Horrigan's shoulder. "You okay, Frank?"

"Yeah . . . now that I'm in on the goddamn gag."

Several of the agents began to laugh, and the rest

joined in; even Campagna smiled.

"Who's the practical joker, anyway?" Horrigan said, rebuttoning his shirt. "Can't a senior citizen take a goddamn nap on his goddamn break?"

Amidst general laughter, the two paramedics mumbled another embarrassed apology and started off; Horrigan called out to them, "Hey, guys—maybe you oughta stick around."

The young paramedic said, "Yeah?"

"Yeah." He scowled at the laughing agents. "You may have a gunshot wound or two to tend to. . . ."

The older paramedic grinned and waved a hand at the air and pulled his younger associate along, as laughter increased and continued, agents standing around the lounge area drinking coffee or soft drinks, enjoying the moment, enjoying having today's Presidential motorcade duty behind them.

Campagna settled his heavy frame onto a chair near Horrigan's. "Serves you right, all the gags you used to pull."

Matt Wilder pulled a chair around. "Yeah—like that deal with that hat!"

"Hat?" Lilly asked. She sat on the edge of Matt's armchair, legs crossed; even under the severe pants suit, those limbs looked shapely.

Matt shook his head, chuckling. "Way back when we were at the St. Louis Field Office together, we had this new supervisor . . . a real jerk. No sense of humor, always breaking everybody's hump."

"Jerian," Horrigan said.

"Yeah! *That* asshole! Art Jerian. Always wore a fucking—'scuse my French, Lilly—hat."

"It's okay, Matt," she said, with a wicked smile. "A little French is apropos after who we guarded today. Go on, go on—'this jerk always wore a fucking hat. . . .' "

Matt continued: "Anyway, Frank goes out and buys a hat just like this guy's—"

"No!" interrupted a grinning Campagna. "Frank buys *four* hats, each one identical to his supervisor's, but different *sizes*. Then he pulls a switch— the first of many."

"I don't get it," Lilly said.

Matt picked up the ball: "See, Frank here tells the jerko boss that the terrible humidity in St. Louis makes your head swell and shrink."

Campagna pitched in gleefully, "So when it was hot, Frank switched the jerk's hat for a smaller one . . . and when it was cold, a *bigger* one."

The various agents milling around were all laughing now. Even Horrigan was smiling, like the naughty kid he was, at heart.

"Don't knock it," Horrigan said. "After three months, the idiot put in for transfer."

The group roared with laughter.

"Last we saw of him," Matt was saying, tears running down his cheeks, "he was leaving the office to catch a plane . . . a little hat sitting on that fat head of his."

"He looked like an organ grinder's monkey!" Campagna howled.

Everybody was laughing now, Horrigan included.

"Ah," Horrigan said. "How I hated that bastard."

"Okay, okay," Campagna said, finally remembering he was the boss; getting up, patting the air, quieting the laughter. "Back to work, everybody. Back to work. . . ."

He lumbered off and so did the other agents, gradually.

Horrigan, however, hadn't moved out of his chair. And pretty Lilly was hanging back, pouring herself a cup of coffee. He watched her admiringly, liking the way her figure made even the most masculine-cut clothes look feminine.

"Who was behind that prank, anyway?" he asked her.

"Maybe it wasn't a prank." She stood in front of him and sipped her coffee. Her gaze was steady—not quite the "stare" yet, perhaps; but intimidating enough to him, right now. "You looked pretty pale out there today. I wouldn't have been surprised to see you keel over."

"Horseshit," Horrigan said. "Anyway, whoever the guy is, I'm gonna get back at him. Probably that prick Watts."

"Could be." She finished her coffee, wadded up the paper cup and tossed it in the trash receptacle. "On the other hand, how can you be sure it was a 'prick' who did it?"

Then she gave him an enigmatic smile and walked back to her desk, putting a little more female swing in her step than he'd seen from her before.

"Cute," he said to himself. "Real cute."

Then he hauled himself up and out of the chair. He had to check in with D'Andrea and see if his partner was getting anywhere on his phone buddy, Booth.

Had Booth been in that crowd today? Horrigan wondered.

Something told him he had.

7

• •

"You missed the turn," Horrigan said.

D'Andrea, behind the wheel of his Pontiac Sunbird, chauffeuring his partner home after dark, winced in irritation. "Oh, man!"

"That's K Street back there," Horrigan said matter-of-factly. He was leafing through the file D'Andrea had prepared on Booth; most of it was familiar to him: summary of the canvassing of the tenants at the apartment house, the goose-egg results of the lab technicians.

"Can you drive?" D'Andrea asked.

"Sure." Horrigan glanced at the official notification that his own apartment had been wiretapped with his permission. "Why?"

"Why? You mean, 'why' as in 'why don't you have your own goddamn car'?"

Shrugging, Horrigan kept flipping through the file folder. "I spent a lot of time in New York. I'm a public transportation kind of guy."

D'Andrea gestured toward his dash. "Does this look

like a bus to you? Do I look like Ralph Kramden?"

Horrigan glanced at his partner and barely smiled. "Retaining water, are we?"

D'Andrea smiled back, reluctantly. "It's just, if you like riding buses, then why d'ya make me take you home every night? It's not exactly on my way."

"Pleasure of your company." Horrigan was staring at Booth's Colorado driver's license, in the name of the long-dead eleven-year-old Joseph McCrawley; the license was paper-clipped to the inside back of the manila folder.

"I can turn around up here," D'Andrea said, then noticed Horrigan staring at the photo on the license.

D'Andrea shook his head. "Some kinda weirdo, huh?"

Booth had light hair combed down over a high forehead, with matching beard and light gray eyes. High cheekbones, small chin—the skull beneath the skin was spookily apparent.

"*Some* kind of weirdo, all right," Horrigan said softly. Then it hit him; his eyes tightened with thought, and he said, "But *what* kind?"

"Huh?" D'Andrea asked, looking over curiously at his now bright-eyed partner.

"Don't turn around yet," Horrigan said, sitting forward, pointing up the street. "There's a newsstand on the next corner . . . pull up."

The store on the corner was a modern, all-night operation featuring out-of-town papers, paperbacks, magazines—everything from *Pravda* to *Hustler*. Horrigan was looking for neither. He walked quickly along, eyes skimming across colorful covers of all kinds, their slick surfaces reflecting the bright overhead lighting. Specialty magazines of every stripe stretched out before him; and then he spotted what he was after, and smiled.

He crouched and thumbed through several of the hobby and model-kit-collecting mags before selecting one with a familiar cover: the current *Model Car Collector.*

An issue of this magazine had been on top of a stack of similar magazines resting on Booth's bureau, back at the seedy apartment; and on that stack of magazines had rested a sleek, futuristic scale-model vehicle.

Soon he was back in D'Andrea's front seat, pointing to a similar futuristic model car that graced the *Model Car Collector* cover, saying, "The one in Booth's apartment was just like this! Or damn near."

D'Andrea, behind the wheel of the parked car, frowned skeptically. "How is *that* a clue? Which is what you seem to think it is."

Horrigan grinned. "You said he was a weirdo, right? And I asked, what *kind*—remember?"

"Sure."

He slapped the magazine cover. "*This* kind. He's a model-car collector. Hobby-kit nut."

"So?"

"So," Horrigan said, gesturing impatiently, "it's a place to start. Turn this thing around—drop me off at my apartment, I want to call this in right away."

D'Andrea rolled his eyes a little, shook his head, said, "Sure, Frank—you're the boss, Frank," and did as he was told.

Within minutes D'Andrea was off to his wife and kid in the Virginia suburbs, and Horrigan was in his tiny apartment, seated in his easy chair. He hadn't even bothered powering up Miles Davis in the CD player; he was on the phone, with the first available on-duty agent at the Washington field office.

"I want you to send some agents around to check out how these kits are sold," he was saying. "Looking through this magazine, I'd say they sell 'em mostly mail-order. And probably some specialty shops. These kits are limited editions, so tracing—"

Call Waiting click-clicked in his ear.

"Hold on a second," he said, "I got another call coming in. . . . Just wait, I'll dump whoever it is. . . ."

He tapped the hook and said, impatiently, "Yeah?"

"Hello, Frank."

The whisper-soft, almost melodic voice was unmistakable.

"Well, Booth," Horrigan said, sitting up, "how are ya doin'?"

"Why, I'm fine, Frank. How are you?"

"I'm swell—look hang on, just let me get rid of this other call—" He clicked the hook and said hurriedly, "You guys got him?"

"We got him," the agent said. "You know what you have to do."

Keep him on the line.

Horrigan smiled tightly as he clicked back to Booth, who said, almost sweetly, "I hope you're not trying to trace me, Frank."

"How could I do that?"

"You could have had your friends come in and tap your line."

"Ah, I didn't bother. Didn't figure you'd have the nerve to call back."

"Oh, you bothered, Frank. And you knew I'd call again. I think you also know that one thing I *don't* lack is nerve."

"What *do* you lack?"

"Oh . . . many things. Many things were taken away from me, over the years. Just like you, Frank. You lost so much. We both have. I hope the years haven't taken *too* bad a toll on you, because I was looking forward to having a . . . worthwhile adversary."

"Were you, now?"

"Yes. Speaking of which, how *are* you?" The gentle voice seemed to convey genuine concern. "I was worried about you today."

"Really? And why's that, Booth?"

"In the motorcade . . . I thought you were going to faint dead away, Frank." There was a *tch-tch* sound; the sarcasm behind the sympathy was coming through now. "You really should have gotten yourself back into tip-top shape before asking back on the Protective detail."

Horrigan's hand was gripping the phone, veins looking about to burst. But he kept his voice placid: "You know, Booth, maybe you're right. Maybe I am out of shape."

"You were in wonderful shape, once upon a time. By the way, I've got your movie on my TV right now."

"Movie?"

"Are you a movie buff, Frank? Do you know what an *auteur* is?"

"No."

"That's a French word for 'author,' but it's used to refer to truly distinctive directors, like, oh . . . Hitchcock. Leone. Truffaut."

First the Beatles, then model cars, now movies.

"I was never in a movie," Horrigan said.

"Sure you were, Frank! You worked with the most

distinctive *auteur* of them all! His output was small, but his style, the impact of his work . . . indelible. I refer, of course, to that great cinematic genius, Abraham Zapruder."

Horrigan's anger turned to nausea.

"Dallas, November 22, 1963 . . . I know where *I* was—and I know where *you* were, Frank. You were in shape then weren't you? But, sadly, it didn't do you, or *him*, much good—did it?"

Horrigan's tongue was thick in his mouth.

"What *happened* to you that day? Only one agent reacted to the gunfire—and the rest of you, highly trained, your reflexes like coiled springs? Nothing. I keep watching this over and over . . . but you never leave that running board."

"Shut up," he said.

"Frank—no need for hostility. Can't two friends discuss a difficult subject, openly? Now where was I? Ah. You were actually *closer* to Kennedy than the agent who did react—you were closer to him than any of the agents, in more ways than one."

Horrigan had been on the Texas Book Depository side of the follow-up car.

Now Booth was musing rhapsodically. "At night, Frank, in bed, lying there, trying to sleep, what do you see when you dream? Do you dream, Frank? Do you see things, faces, events in your dreams? Do you see that rifle in the window? Do you see Kennedy's head coming apart?"

Horrigan shut his eyes, but it didn't stop the sound of Booth's soothing voice and his biting words. How he wanted to hang up . . . but he had to keep this psycho on the line. . . .

"It must be terrible, Frank, knowing that if you'd

just reacted to that first shot, you could have gotten there in time and put yourself in the line of fire. Of course, then it would've been *your* head that came apart, probably."

Why weren't agents bursting in Booth's door, wrestling him to the floor, snapping his wrists in cuffs?

Booth was saying, "Do you wish you'd been able to give your life for his, Frank?"

Horrigan refused to give him the satisfaction of a straight answer. Instead he merely said, "You can't change history."

"True. How very true. But you know what? You can make it."

That chilled Horrigan more than anything Booth had said yet.

"You lost so much," Booth was saying. "Your wife left you . . . took your little girl. When they interviewed you, for that magazine article . . . the one about the tenth anniversary of the assassination? You were so great. So forthright, so honest. Couldn't have been easy for you to admit your drinking problem publicly, to 'fess up to how hard it must've been to live with you. I bet you thought that would get her back, your wife, didn't you? Saying that."

He flinched at Booth's insight.

"The world can be so unfair, so cruel, to an honest man," Booth said. And this time the soft voice held no discernible sarcasm.

What was taking the agents so fucking long to get to Booth's place and collar him? How the hell was he expected to stay indefinitely cool, to hold back his anger, with this nutcase on the line?

"You know *my* story, Booth. What's yours?"

The *tch-tch* sound again. "Can't tell you, Frank. Sorry."

Then Booth whispered a few bars of "With a Little Help from My Friends," and added, "It's so nice, Frank . . . having a friend."

The phone clicked dead.

A wave of rage, bitterness and confusion washed over Horrigan as he stared at the receiver; then he clicked the hook, got the field-office agent on the line again and demanded, "Well?"

"Take it easy, Horrigan. Hang up and we'll call you when we've got him."

He slammed the phone down, got up, poured himself some Jameson—an inch more than usual—and gulped at it greedily. For the first time in twelve years, he wanted a smoke.

"That fucker," he muttered. "That *fucker*. . . ."

He was pacing, drinking, swearing, when the phone rang again and he grabbed it off the hook and said, "What?"

The field agent sounded both weary and embarrassed. "We had a trace, sent the local cops straight to the address, a working-class neighborhood, where they burst in this little house with their guns in hand."

"And?"

The sigh was also weary and embarrassed. "And they found a teenage couple doin' the nasty on the couch in front of the TV."

"Shit!"

At the Intelligence Division Office, not half an hour later, an electronics technician told Horrigan that the suspect might have had a device that altered the line's voltage slightly, which could make it seem as if he were calling from another number.

"This device, how . . . where . . . would he get it?"

The tech, a thin, balding, bespectacled agent named Carducci, shrugged and said, "If he had the specs, he could build one."

"Where would he get the specs?"

"An electronics magazine." Another shrug. "I could build one myself."

"Great. So if he calls again, we can't trace him?"

"Well . . . we could run a parity check, if he's on a line wired for digital switches."

"Great! So you *can* trace him."

"Not necessarily. Not if he's on an *analog* line."

Horrigan slammed a hand on the desk and made Carducci's computer screen jump. "I don't give a rat's ass about this electronics bullshit. I just want a straight fucking answer! In English!"

Carducci patted the air with both hands, trying to calm Horrigan. "If he calls again, you keep him on the line, and I'll see what I can do. Fair enough?"

Horrigan nodded sullenly.

Carducci lifted a gently warning finger. "But if you pull any local cops in again, or our boys either, better warn 'em not to go busting down any more doors. We don't know *what* this guy is capable of, electronically speaking."

"I already know what he's capable of," Horrigan said, and he wasn't speaking electronically.

Carducci squinted behind the glasses. "What?"

"Any goddamn thing."

8

In the southwest corner of the West Wing of the White House, in one of the several rooms known collectively as the Rectangular Office, the President's chief of staff, Harry Sargent, sat at a conference table with Assistant Director of the Secret Service Campagna and three agents—Bill Watts, Lilly Raines and Frank Horrigan, at whose suggestion the meeting had been held.

In Horrigan's estimation, Sargent was the most unpleasant chief of staff since H. R. Haldeman—and that was saying something. Jack Kennedy had dispensed with the position, saying he didn't want or need an Assistant President. Even that unpleasant son of a bitch Lyndon Johnson had gone without one.

Not the current President, unfortunately.

Looking rumpled in his brown suit with red-and-yellow tie, the heavy-set, fifty-something, Nixon-haired Sargent had been clearly irritated at being bothered. He was, to give the devil his due, in the midst of the final days of a hectic reelection campaign that wasn't going at all well.

But now, listening to a tape of Horrigan's phone conversation with Booth the night before, Sargent seemed intrigued.

"*I bet you thought that would get her back, your wife*," Booth's voice was saying from the cassette player, "*didn't you?*"

Hearing this stuff again, in the presence of these others—including that prick Watts—sent needles through the agent's brain; Booth's rantings about Horrigan's personal life, and his professional failure at Dallas. . . .

But Horrigan kept his face immobile. Once, for a moment, his eyes locked with Lilly's—she seemed embarrassed for him, her gaze warmly compassionate.

It didn't help.

Interest flagging, Sargent looked impatiently at his watch as Booth's disembodied voice was saying, "*It's so nice, Frank, having a friend.*"

Campagna reached over and shut off the cassette player.

"That's it?" Sargent asked.

"That's it."

Though it wasn't particularly hot in the impressive suite of offices, Sargent mopped his red-mottled face with a handkerchief.

His reaction was typically rude: "What the hell does this have to do with me?"

Campagna, hands folded prayerfully, leaned forward, earnestly. "Harry—we'd like you to consider canceling the President's dinner tomorrow night."

Sargent's eyes flared. "The *state* dinner? At the

French Embassy? Are you people out of your minds?"

"We take this individual very seriously," Campagna said. "We've already classified him a 'lookout.'"

"Bill?" Sargent said, eyes narrowed. "What do you think?"

"I agree with Sam," Watts said flatly, going up a point in Horrigan's book.

The red-faced chief of staff sighed heavily. "I understand you have three or four hundred such individuals classified that way," he said, with a humorless smirk. "They're all at large, and yet we're not canceling any state dinners over *them*. What makes *this* lunatic any different?"

Watts didn't answer. Campagna looked at Horrigan and nodded for him to pick up the ball and carry it.

"*This* lunatic," Horrigan said, "manipulated the phone lines in a disturbingly sophisticated manner. In addition, he's a skilled builder of model cars."

Sargent was looking at the agent with the dismayed, disgusted expression of a vegetarian presented with a cheeseburger. "Model cars?"

"Well, yes," Horrigan said. "Some of which operate by remote control, further indicating electronics expertise—"

"For this," Sargent said with blunt sarcasm, "you want me to alter the itinerary of the world's most powerful man, and offend forty million Frenchmen in the bargain?"

Horrigan tried again. "With skills of this kind, if Booth has any knowledge of explosives—"

"You guys do your job," Sargent interrupted curtly, "and there won't be any problem."

"We are doing our job," Horrigan said, just as curtly. "That's what we're doing by advising you to cancel."

Lilly, who seemed uneasy with so much animosity in the air, gestured with a reasonable open hand. "Protocol limits our effectiveness at an embassy, sir."

"She's right," Horrigan said. "Smuggling in weapons at an embassy, even with our best efforts, is a piece of cake. . . ."

Sargent was shaking his head in disbelief; his expression was almost contemptuous. "What the hell are you trying to say? That now you think the *French* want to bump off the President?"

Sargent's disdain was withering; the agents shifted uncomfortably in their chairs. Except for Horrigan.

"Just once," Horrigan said quietly, temper bubbling, "I'd like to meet a White House chief of staff that didn't fight the Secret Service every goddamn step of the way."

Sargent's eyes flared again, and Horrigan—getting a stern sideways glare from Campagna, noticing Watts cringing in embarrassment, Lilly wincing—knew he'd overstepped. Not that he cared.

The bulky Sargent, his bulldog face tight, pointed at the tape player. "You know what *I* think, Agent Horrigan? I think this screwball touched a raw nerve or two, where you're concerned. And now you're overreacting."

Horrigan gave the chief of staff the same zombie stare he would give a crowd around the Presidential limo.

He said coldly, "I'm just trying to protect your boss."

"What the hell do you think *I'm* doing!" Sargent dropped his mask for a moment and the frazzled man behind it peeked out; this guy had Potomac fever so bad he might croak from it.

"Latest polls have us trailing by twelve goddamn points," Sargent said glumly. "If I don't pull off a couple miracles, and quick, I'm maybe not going to *have* a boss—he's gonna be out of a job in six weeks, and so will I."

Sargent slammed a fist into a palm.

He said, "I have to get the President out in front of the people where he can be *seen*, damn it."

"Maybe you were right, at that," Horrigan said.

"What?"

"Maybe pretty soon you're not going to have a boss, or a job."

Campagna covered his eyes, wearily.

Sargent sat up, spat words. "What the hell's that supposed to mean?"

Horrigan shrugged. "You can't work for a dead man."

That chilled the room, but just momentarily. There was an agenda of Secret Service–related matters to go over with the White House, and Sargent brusquely turned to Sam and said, "Next order of business."

And that was that.

At that moment, elsewhere in the city, in a dank, dark basement apartment, Mitch Leary—in T-shirt and jeans—worked in blessed stillness as he toiled away joyfully in his workshop.

Sitting at his workbench, he spread out before him the tools of his hobby (although it had become something more than just a hobby, hadn't it?). Neatly arranged around the modest pegboard-lined work area were bottles of paint, tubes of glue, magnifying lenses, varied grades of sandpaper (mostly very fine), jars of wax, assorted drills.

Also laid out neatly before him were various pieces of metal. Assembled, they formed a small, square automatic handgun. Disassembled, he would recast them, in hand-made molds, using a resin of his own design. Most resins were brittle. Not this one.

Not this one.

He hummed his favorite Beatles tune as he aligned before him various small pieces of hand-cut wood. Then he began unwrapping plastic-covered sticks of green modeling clay—they were like sticks of butter, but of course of a thicker consistency.

He began working with the clay, pressing it onto each of the little wooden platforms, applying a good, green thickness. Still humming, he lifted the barrel of the automatic and pressed it onto his clay-covered platform, pushing it down in.

The process was called claying up, in the modeling game.

But of course, Leary wasn't making a *model* gun.

And this was for another game entirely.

9

The French Embassy was just one of many mansions in Kalorama, the prestigious neighborhood northwest of Dupont Circle. Tonight, Secret Service agents stood guard along the drive that curved beyond the pillared, wrought-iron fence as dignitaries, socialites and their significant others entered the massive, ornately detailed brick structure in a blur of furs, gowns, jewelry and tuxes. Among the classy crowd, dressed to blend in at this black-tie affair, were a score more of special agents.

One of these was Horrigan, not terribly at ease in formal attire even after years of occasional duty like this. Another was Lilly Raines, dressed to kill in a black satin, rather low-cut gown. At work she wore her reddish-blond hair up; tonight, it revealed itself, brushing creamy, lightly freckled shoulders. For some reason, the lovely sight of her made Horrigan feel almost sad. She stirred something in him that he preferred to leave slumbering.

They were on either side of the guest-lined dance floor in the ballroom. Though neither wore the "zombie" stare (not appropriate in a gathering such as this), both agents were constantly examining the faces in the crowd; several times their darting eyes met, and Horrigan thought he detected a faintly etched line of a smile on the redhead's full, scarlet-lipsticked lips.

At the moment, the President and his radiant First Lady were moving through the throng with the President of France, shaking hands, chatting briefly with this guest and that one, half-encircled by agents including Matt Wilder and Bill Watts, the latter staying closer to the President than the First Lady.

The orchestra began to play a syrupy rendition of "With a Little Help from My Friends," which unnerved Horrigan. *Booth's* favorite song, of all things—the irrational notion that Booth might have somehow arranged it to happen nibbled at Horrigan's brain.

As couples moved out onto the dance floor, including the President and First Lady, Horrigan angled across to where Lilly stood.

"Odd choice of tunes, isn't it?" Horrigan said.

Lilly, having to speak up over the music, said, "It's out of tribute to the President. He's a Baby Boomer—everybody knows the Beatles are his favorite group."

"He isn't alone," Horrigan said sourly.

"What?"

"Nothing."

Between songs, he smiled at her and said, "You look lovely tonight."

"Well, thank you."

"Good enough to eat."

Her smirk was teasing. "Every time I start to sympathize with you, you have to make some inappropriate, sexist remark, don't you?"

"I'll try to make my next sexist remark an appropriate one." Then he frowned and said, "What do you mean, 'sympathize'?"

She glanced away. "You know," she said awkwardly.

"No, I don't know."

"That . . . tape of your phone call. When Booth started talking about your wife . . ."

"Ex-wife."

"Well. Anyway, I felt . . . sorry."

"Sorry *for* me, you mean?"

"Forget it." Her mouth went firm and she turned away, still inspecting the guests. "You know, you can be aggravating as hell, Horrigan."

He rocked on his heels as the orchestra began to play an equally syrupy rendition of George Harrison's "Something."

"I'm sure getting a lot of sympathy these days," he said. "First from a deranged wanna-be assassin . . . now from a pretty girl I aggravate."

She looked at him, more amused than offended. "Girl?"

"Woman. Person. Whatever. Politically correct is tough for a guy my age. Look, uh . . . why don't we blend in . . . you know. Dance."

She shook her head. "I don't think so. I can keep an eye out better from the sidelines. Maybe some other time . . . when we're off duty."

"We're off duty in a couple hours."

She looked away. "No thanks."

He took out his irritation by kidding her. He stared wolfishly at her low-cut dress.

"What are you doing, Horrigan?"

"Using my detective abilities. I'm a trained investigator, you know."

"What are you talking about?"

He nodded to himself, as if he'd just come up with a particularly shrewd deduction. "I think I finally figured out where you carry your service revolver . . ."

But now she wasn't amused. She glared at him, and he shrugged and moved off into the crowd.

He didn't see her glare turn into a smile, but Bill Watts did, disapprovingly, turning Lilly's face properly Secret Service sober.

The next day, on a flight to Los Angeles, Mitch Leary—traveling under the name James Carney— sat in First Class, humming "With a Little Help from My Friends" as he made out a personal check on his lowered tray table. In the amount of $1,000, on a personalized Microspan Corporation check, it was made out to "The President's Reelection Campaign."

Leary adjusted his glasses; he wore a tailored business suit, had full dark hair and mustache, to all outward appearances a pleasant-looking middle-aged executive in transit. He held the check before him, his "James Carney" signature glistening wetly, and smiled at what he'd done, as if he'd just painted an exquisite landscape.

The pilot's voice was on the speaker, announcing their imminent arrival in Los Angeles, where it was currently a pleasant seventy-five degrees.

"Could you put your tray table up, sir?" the attractive female flight attendant asked nicely as she passed by.

He smiled sweetly at her, said, "Certainly," placing the check in a stamped envelope. He sealed it, tucked it in his inside suit-coat pocket and put up his tray table.

West Executive Drive, the closed-off street between the West Wing of the White House and the Old Executive Office Building, was a blacktop with marked-off, numbered parking spaces. Some of them were designated for the limousines of visiting officials; others belonged to the staff of either adjacent building. Lilly Raines was walking toward her late-model Buick, parked at the far end of the lot, when Horrigan called out to her.

"Agent Raines!"

It was two days after the uneventful state dinner at the French Embassy, a beautiful, nicely cool autumn evening.

He jogged up to her, grinned in what he hoped was still a boyish manner; at his age, he couldn't be sure.

"How would you like to give a colleague a lift home?" he said. "My partner D'Andrea's already left for the day."

She gave him a hard stare.

"You're getting better at it," he said.

"At what?"

"The 'stare.'"

Her blank expression crinkled into a grin. "Why do you insist on hitting on me?"

"Hitting on you? Is that what I'm doing? Whatever happened to flirting?"

"Anita Hill," she said, and worked a key in the driver's side car door. Speaking over her shoulder, she said, "You know this relationship can't go anywhere, so why do you keep at it?"

"This is encouraging."

"What is?"

"Hearing that we have a relationship. Come on, give me a ride. Be a pal."

She glanced back, weakening.

"I'll buy you an ice-cream cone, little girl."

She raised an eyebrow and he put up his hands, as if to show he was unarmed, and tried the boyish look again.

This time it took.

She laughed, and it was a rippling, full-throated laugh, as nice and cool as the breeze. "Get in, you big lug."

Soon they were sitting against a marble column on the steps of the Lincoln Memorial, licking ice-cream cones. No one else was around; no tourists, nobody. Just a gentle breeze that riffled her pinned-up hair.

"I wish you'd let that down," he said.

"What?"

"That hair of yours."

She grinned her crinkly grin, licked the cone. "Let's not get ahead of ourselves, Horrigan."

"Make it 'Frank,' would you? I'm tired of calling you Agent Raines."

"Okay, Frank."

"Thanks, Lilly." He licked the cone; he had vanilla, she had chocolate. "Y'know, I never worked with a female agent before. How many are there, anyway?"

"Hundred and twenty-six, last count."

He laughed once, deep in his chest. "Window dressing."

She half-frowned. "What do you mean?"

"No offense, but a hundred twenty-six out of thirty-five hundred . . . you're window dressing. Having you around makes the Prez look good to the feminist voters."

She smirked at him. "Is that the 'appropriate' sexist remark you promised me, the other night?"

"It's not sexist. Get real, Lil—half the shit we do is window dressing. Men damn well included."

"I don't believe that."

"Really? How 'bout us running alongside an armored limo that'd take an antitank missile to dent?" He laughed his deep, mildly derisive laugh again. "We're there for show. To make the President look presidential."

She was biting at her cone now, crunching at it with tiny perfect white teeth. "Oh yeah? Well, if I'm here to court the feminist vote, what the hell demographics do *you* represent?"

He thought about it, crunched at his own cone, grinned at her triumphantly. "The white-piano-playing-heterosexuals-over-fifty contingent. We may be small in number, but we got a hell of a powerful lobby."

She granted him a little laugh; she'd finished her cone. Glancing at her watch, she rose and said, "Time flies when you're being aggravated."

"I guess so. Where you headed in such a hurry?"

"I have a date."

"Anybody I know?"

"Nobody that's any of your damn business." That apparently came off harsher than she'd meant it to; she softened it with a smile and said, "You want that ride, now?"

He was still working at the cone. "Naw. Think I'll stick around. I kinda like the way the light hits old Abe round this time of day."

She looked up at the monument, then at Horrigan, and nodded. "Bye. Thanks for the ice cream."

"No obligation, little girl."

She gave him half a wave and walked toward her car, parked on the street; beyond her, he could see the Reflecting Pool and the Washington Monument, serene, postcard perfect.

If she looks back, he thought, *she's interested*.

She kept walking.

Come on, Lil. . . . Turn around. . . .

She neared the car.

Just one little backward glance . . . I don't care if it's smug, just so you look. . . .

He was ready to give up when she touched her car door, and sneaked a little glance back at him, over her shoulder.

He beamed at her, waved.

She looked away, chagrined, and got in the car.

Horrigan crunched his last bite of cone, feeling better about himself than he had in days. Weeks. Months. He leaned back on the marble steps where he had once done duty guarding Martin Luther King, the night of the "I have a dream" oration. He turned to look with admiration at the brooding, twenty-foot likeness of a President whose last days included creating the

Secret Service, but who never had any such protection himself.

"Wish I coulda been there for ya, big guy," Horrigan said, only half-kidding.

After a while, he walked to the nearest bus stop.

10

Mitch Leary, still hiding behind glasses and a business executive's persona, pulled his rental Buick Park Avenue into a slot along a major thoroughfare in Santa Monica. Briefcase in hand, he smiled up at the gently waving palm trees lining the street. The balmy weather soothed him. It was almost like being on vacation.

Almost.

He entered the Southwest Bank and went to the Customer Service teller. According to the nameplate along the side of her window, she was Pam Magnus —blond, mid-thirties, slightly overweight, compensating with a little too much makeup and a black-and-white vertically striped shirtdress. Right now she was working on her computer, and she smiled cheerfully and said, "Just a moment, sir."

Leary returned the smile easily. "No rush."

But she was done almost immediately and her eyes were bright, her manner genuinely upbeat. "And how may I help you?"

He pushed a cashier's check in the amount of sixty thousand dollars across the counter to her.

"I'd like to open a corporate account," he said, "and deposit this." He'd given cash for the cashier's check at a San Jose bank.

"Certainly," she said. "I'll need to see your corporate resolutions . . ."

"Of course." He propped his briefcase up on the counter, popped it open, got out the paperwork, snapped the briefcase shut and passed the papers to her with another bland smile.

He watched her type "MICROSPAN CORPORATION" onto her computer screen as she read from the top sheet. She paused to blow her nose, gave him another pleasant glance as she continued rapidly touching fingers to keyboard.

Chitchatting, she said, "What sort of business is Microspan, Mr. Carney?"

"Computer software."

"Up in San Jose, I see."

"That's right." He adjusted the glasses on the bridge of his nose. "We're based there. I'm here to open the L.A. branch office."

Still typing, she grinned and said, "I always did like that song."

"Pardon?"

" 'Do You Know the Way to San Jose?' "

"Oh. That is a nice song."

She was a talkative little thing; kind of attractive. Was she flirting with him? Leary felt flattered, though he realized it was a well-off business executive she was coming on to.

"San Jose really is a terrific place," she said. "Are you from there, originally?"

"No."

She glanced away from the screen as she typed, batted her eyes at him. "Where *are* you from?"

"Minneapolis."

Her face exploded into an even bigger smile. "No kidding! So am I."

Not good.

"Small world," he said.

She returned her gaze to her glowing green screen. "Didn't you just *hate* those winters! Nine months a year, I'd burrow inside and pig out." She made a face, rolled her eyes. "I moved here and lost thirty pounds."

"Congratulations."

Chirpily, she asked, "What high school did you go to?"

Thinking quickly, he said, "New Brighton."

"New Brighton High?"

"That's right."

She looked at him curiously, fingers halted over the keys. "But there isn't any New Brighton High."

He smiled noncommittally. "There was back when I graduated."

She seemed to study him now, her eyes like a raccoon's behind all that makeup; maybe she was trying to figure out how old he was, to enroll him in some mythical New Brighton High that had been before her time. . . .

Then she shrugged and turned back to her computer and her fingers again began to fly.

She said, "Maybe I'm just confused." She smirked self-mockingly. "That happens a lot."

Shit! Shit shit shit. He was tapping his foot; willed himself to stop. *Okay, then,* he thought, *change of plan. Improvise and adapt* . . . He looked at her hands. No wedding ring. Good. He craned his neck just a bit, not suspiciously he hoped, and saw a photo on her desk: a pet German shepherd. A dog, not a boyfriend.

Good.

"You certainly have a pleasant way about you," he said affably.

She turned from the screen to beam at him. "Why, thank you, Mr. Carney. . . ."

When they had completed his transaction, he walked away slowly.

If I look back at her, he thought, *she may sense my concern. . . .*

But he had to look back.

I think *I* won *her over,* he thought. *But I have to be sure. . . .*

At the door, he glanced back, and she was watching him; her expression was plainly troubled. He smiled at her, nodded, waved cordially, and she smiled back.

But the smile was forced.

He went to his rental Buick, sat on the driver's side with a blank face behind which thoughts buzzed and bubbled and brewed. Then, with sudden force, he slammed the heel of one hand into the steering wheel.

"Shit," he said softly.

How could such a beautiful day go so wrong?

Late that afternoon, just down the block from Southwest Bank, Leary sat in an Olds Cutlass he'd rented an hour before, under another of his names. Despite the change of car, the Carney persona remained—glasses, suit-and-tie, dark hair and mustache. Windows down, he enjoyed the tropical breeze. Hummed his Beatles tune. Waited.

Finally, she exited, waving to someone still within.

He watched pleasantly plump Pam Magnus, in her vertically striped black-and-white dress, walk with the heavy gait of the end of the workday, to the bank's parking lot.

Moments later, in a red Honda Civic, she pulled out into traffic.

So, discreetly, did he.

She led him to Ocean Park, to a small white clapboard house on a quiet side street in the sort of vaguely rundown neighborhood that could be considered cool, or seedy, depending on your point of view. Leary found it rather charming. Funky, even. Not a bad place to live.

He rolled by as she walked up a cracked walk to her door, where she was greeted by deep, almost ferocious barking.

"How's my baby?" she called.

That damn German shepherd in the picture, he'd bet; he went on by, drove a few blocks and came up on the opposite side of the street, where he parked half a block down. He sat quietly chewing his thumbnail.

Then he got out of the car, not pausing for traffic, and crossed, almost skipping up the cracked walk to the porch of the little house. Glancing around at neighboring houses, he saw no sign of anyone watching.

He knocked.

The dog began barking, and he could hear the

woman's muffled voice saying, "Rory, be quiet! Be good!"

The dog had quieted by the time the door cracked open, and a distracted-looking Pam Magnus looked out; she was nibbling on a chocolate-chip cookie. She frowned, not recognizing him at first; then she did, and the cookie disappeared behind her back, as if she'd been caught at something.

"Mr. Carney . . . what . . ."

"I'm sorry to just drop by on you like this, Miss Magnus."

She frowned in confusion. "How did you find me, Mr. Carney?"

Smiled. Shrugged. "I just looked you up in the phone book."

Her frown turned frightened. "I'm not listed," she blurted.

She began to close the door and he stopped it with his hand. But he tried to keep his smile as unthreatening as possible.

"I guess I better make a clean breast of it," he said embarrassedly. "This is going to sound bad, but . . . I followed you home. I admit it."

"Mr. Carney . . ."

"I tried, at the bank, to work up the nerve to ask you to join me for dinner, but . . . just couldn't. Then, on an impulse, I followed you."

"That's, uh, very sweet," she said nervously, pushing on the door.

He held it firmly open. "I don't know anyone in L.A., and I do hate eating alone. . . ."

"Please, Mr. Carney. I'm busy."

He half-smiled, made his expression sheepish. "Also, I wanted to apologize for lying to you. We both know I'm not from Minneapolis."

"I . . . I shouldn't have bothered you with so many personal questions. Please, I *am* busy. . . ."

He pushed the door open, and she gasped, and suddenly he was inside. He glanced around the low-ceilinged little living room, with its pink stucco walls, waxy bare wood floors, arched doorways, discount-store furnishings and Starving Artist seascapes.

"Where's your dog?" he asked. "I heard him barking."

"Out back. You better go. I'll scream."

His smile turned sad; he shook his head. "Scream? This isn't like that. In just a moment, I'll go. But I just want to make sure there was no misunderstanding about how I . . . misled you at the bank. By the way, you didn't mention our conversation to anyone else there, did you?"

"No. . . . Mr. Carney, you're scaring me. I have to ask you to leave . . . *now*. . . ."

"Pam," another voice called, a female voice, "who are you talking to in there? Is it Dave? I thought I was supposed to meet him at—"

A young woman entered from a bedroom, a slender, borderline attractive brunette with a nice body in a short drop-dead red dress: she had a white clutch purse in one hand.

"Oh," she said to Leary. Then she smiled and gave Pam a sly look, apparently pleased to see her pudgy roommate entertaining a guy. "Hi. You're not Dave."

"No I'm not."

Pam, edgily, said, "This is my roommate, Sally. Sally, this is Mr. Carney. I opened an account for him today."

"Call me Jim," he said pleasantly.

"Well, it's nice to meet you, Jim," Sally said, just the faintest bit flirtatious. "But I have a date tonight."

Sally smiled again, moving to the door, but Leary stepped in front of her, like a crossing guard.

"Sorry, ladies," he said, "but I just can't let you leave."

"What?" Sally said, with a laugh, and the laugh caught, and gurgled, as his hands clutched her throat, and twisted in opposite directions.

The crack wasn't that loud—like a chiropractic adjustment—but Sally's eyes were wide and her tongue lolling as she, in her drop-dead red dress, dropped dead to the floor.

Personable Pam Magnus had time only to say, "My God," her eyes huge as he quickly did the same to her.

Then the two women were just a pair of limp rag dolls, one scattered here, one scattered there, in the nondescript little living room. The red dress was like a splash of blood, but there was no blood.

"If only you hadn't been from Minneapolis," he told Pam with something approaching regret; but Pam, eyes still huge but nothing in them, of course did not reply. The chocolate-chip cookie was still in her limp hand.

He wasn't proud of himself, exactly, but he was pleased by how fast he'd performed. Unlike Frank Horrigan, the years hadn't taken the edge off Leary's training. The dog had begun to bark out there, possibly hearing something, more likely just sensing it, and Leary was glad he hadn't had to deal with the animal.

Killing a dog was nothing he would have relished.

Just as he was leaving, wiping clean the place on

the door he'd touched, the phone rang. He went over to the answering machine on an end table and clicked it on with a knuckle.

The caller was persistent, and the machine kicked in: "Hi . . . this is Sally," one voice said, while another giggled in the background.

Then the giggly voice said, "And this is Pam. . . ."

And Sally jumped back in to say: "We're either out having fun . . ."

And Pam said, "Or home taking a nap!"

"I'd say the latter," Leary dryly told the quiet room, smiling faintly; he always had time to savor irony.

Dave was leaving a message for Sally as Leary went out.

The street remained quiet. He went to his rental car, and drove with the windows down, enjoying the balmy breeze that ruffled the hair of his black toupee, rustled the leaves of palm trees. It was almost like being on vacation.

Almost.

11

• •

Several days after the two Santa Monica murders, of which he knew nothing, Horrigan was sitting at the desk he'd been assigned in the Presidential Protective Division bullpen when the phone rang. Reading over the President's itinerary for the coming few days, Horrigan reached casually for the phone. From where he sat, he could see both the bank of screens monitoring the White House, and he could see the West Wing itself, across the West Executive Drive parking area.

"Horrigan," he said.

"Frank?"

Booth.

Horrigan half-stood, waving frantically at the other agents around him; Lilly was the first to notice, and he mouthed, "It's him," and then said into the phone, calmly, almost warmly, "Well, Booth."

"I hope you don't mind me calling you at the office," the gentle, almost wispy voice replied. "It's just . . . well, I was in the neighborhood, and didn't think it would be right *not* to touch base."

When not speaking, Horrigan covered the phone mouthpiece, to mask the scurry of activity in the bullpen, in response to this call. Other agents—including Lilly, and Al D'Andrea, who had dropped by to check in with Horrigan—swarmed around his desk, while at another desk nearby, electronics tech Carducci kicked in an array of electronics and taping equipment assembled in anticipation of just such a contingency.

"Always good to hear from you, Booth," Horrigan was saying.

"You don't mind? My calling you at the office, I mean? I don't mean to overstep."

"You kidding? Hey, if you're in the neighborhood, drop on by."

Lilly, Al and others were slipping on headsets provided by intense Jack Okura from Intelligence Division, who was assisting Carducci.

"I'd really like to, Frank," Booth was saying, "in fact, I'd like that a lot. Meeting you is . . . well, it's something I've thought about a lot."

"Really."

"Sure. After all . . . we have so much in common."

Sam Campagna, alerted by the commotion, barreled out of his office and nudged in next to Lilly, Okura handing him a headset.

"What could you and I have in common, Booth? I just don't see it—no offense meant."

"You *should* see it. It's so clear. Plain as day."

"Yeah?"

He could sense Booth's shrug.

"We're both willing to give up our lives for the President," Booth said.

Swallowing, Horrigan looked up at the agents listening in; their expressions were grave.

"We're both honest men, capable men," Booth continued, "who were betrayed by people we trusted."

"I don't remember anybody betraying me."

"Sure they did, Frank! What about the goddamn Warren Commission? They called your procedures 'seriously deficient.' Now, that just wasn't called for."

A migraine-like spear of pain lashed through Horrigan's brain; Lilly was giving him her sympathetic look again, and Sam looked sorrowful. Horrigan looked away, stared at his desk top while he listened to this madman's shit.

"They criticized you, and the other agents," Booth was saying, in a bizarre combination of empathy and scorn, "for going out drinking the night before. As if Kennedy would be alive today, if Frank Horrigan had just been tucked in bed at ten P.M.! Why, it's simply ludicrous."

"Maybe they were right," Horrigan said, meaning it.

"No, no, Frank . . . it's nonsense. You wanted the President to use the bubbletop on his limo. You *begged* your friend . . . 'Jack, Jack . . . '—I can hear you saying it—'Jack, you gotta let us station agents on the bumpers and sideboards of your goddamn limo!' But no. He was a politician, our fair-haired handsome boy."

Horrigan shot a hard look at Carducci at the bank of electronics gear, raising his eyebrows in a plea, as if to say, *Haven't you traced this fucking call yet?*

Carducci, in his headset, nodded back reassuringly, as if to say, *We're getting there, we're getting there.*

"He wouldn't let you do the right thing, would he, your friend Jack? He should have known. He knew he wasn't Mr. Popularity in Texas. He knew at least half a dozen groups wanted him dead. You know what I think, Frank?"

Reluctantly, he asked: "What do you think, Booth?"

"I think he had a death wish. I think he wanted to die, like his older brother Joe died, heroically. Joe was the old man's favorite, right? I think Jack didn't care that his death would ruin your life . . . that it would send the country reeling. No. He was a selfish bastard. His own self-glory was his own, his only, interest. What do you think, Frank? Hmmm?"

Horrigan's heart was trying to pound its way out of his chest; he thought of Harry Sargent's smug comment about the buttons Booth knew to push in him. Sargent was right. Horrigan had to stay calm.

"Well, you're entitled to your opinion, Booth," he said, and glared at Carducci, who patted the air calmingly, mouthing, "Just a few seconds."

Lilly was biting her knuckle; her eyes looked wet.

"I think it's more than just an opinion, Frank. You were betrayed, like I was betrayed."

"Well, who betrayed you, then?"

Horrigan heard Carducci say to Okura, very softly, "I don't think he's scrambled it . . ."

Booth's voice continued in Horrigan's ear, in its terrible soothing way: "Some of the same people, Frank. Some of the same people who betrayed you . . . they betrayed me, too. It's part of what links us. But you know what, Frank? I don't get mad—I get even."

"Even?"

"I'll have my day in the sun, all right. Question is . . . will you have yours?"

"Who says I want one, Booth?"

"You know what I think?" He made the *tch tch* sound. "I think you're in for a *lot* more emotional pain. . . ."

Horrigan squeezed his hand tight over the mouthpiece. In the harshest of whispers, he growled at Carducci: "How the fuck much longer do I have to put up with this crap?"

Carducci's eyes lighted up. "Jesus!" he blurted. Then, sotto voce, he said, "He's right across the street! Lafayette Park! Keep him on!"

The bullpen came alive; Campagna was on the phone, giving whispered orders, agents were scurrying for their coats, their guns.

"Booth?" Horrigan asked.

A dial tone, as taunting as Booth's wispy voice, buzzed in Horrigan's ear.

He threw the receiver on the desk and bolted for the door, pushing to the front of the pack. Footsteps slapping the marble floor and echoing through the ancient corridor, Horrigan, with D'Andrea, Lilly and two other agents in close pursuit, stormed down the hall, damn near knocking over somebody's bewildered-looking, near-elderly secretary.

Revolver in hand, its nose pointing upward, Horrigan flew down the granite steps of the O.E.O.B., the other agents right behind him; at the bottom, five uniformed Secret Service agents joined the team. The cool autumn air felt good, like an invigorating splash of water; heart pounding, Horrigan could smell victory—he could nail this bastard, *now!*

With Horrigan staying in the lead, the group rushed out into Pennsylvania Avenue, one of the uniformed men playing impromptu traffic cop, without a whistle, as cars screeched to halts and drivers yelled curses.

But as he sprinted into the park, Horrigan saw no one up ahead, no one moving quickly, or behaving suspiciously: the usual ungainly mix of ragtag homeless and business-suited workers taking a break from the O.E.O.B., or any of half a dozen other government buildings nearby.

What he'd just put his body through suddenly caught up with him, and he slowed, tried to catch his breath; cool day or not, sweat was running into his eyes. He brushed it away and surveyed the scene. The other agents were rushing to the phone booth at the far end of the park; the White House made an impressive backdrop as they sealed it off.

For what good it would do: again, an abandoned receiver dangled and spun.

Lilly and the others began the hopeless task of questioning the homeless onlookers, while Horrigan strode through the center of the peaceful park, past the statue of Andrew Jackson riding a rearing horse, waving his military hat like Roy Rogers, a cannon on guard nearby.

He's still here, Horrigan thought. *I can smell the son of a bitch. . . .*

His eyes slowly scanned, searching, searching, and finally lighted on an intense man who stood just across from the park, just across H Street. Another of the homeless? The guy was typically unkempt, hippie-ish, in long blond hair, faded denim jacket, ripped jeans, tennies, tie-dye shirt.

Horrigan frowned. Maybe this guy looked just a little *too* hippie-ish. . . .

The latter-day hippie glanced at Horrigan and Horrigan locked onto him with the stare.

It froze the guy.

The hippie stared back for a long moment, licked his lips, turned and began to walk brusquely off, around the corner, down Sixteenth Street.

Horrigan crossed and walked after him, not running, but moving quickly. The hippie turned, gave Horrigan a furtive glance, and quickened his pace.

"I got you, now," Horrigan said, smiling tightly. "I got you now."

He was running when he shouted, "That's our boy!"

Other agents joined in on the chase, but Horrigan was way out in front, summoning energy from some goddamn where, and the hippie, who was Booth, his blond hair flapping like the wig that it was, dashed into the street, where a taxi, blaring its horn, slammed on its brakes, but not quite in time.

Horrigan winced, hoping it had clipped Booth just hard enough . . . for some reason, he preferred that the asshole remain alive, just now . . . but the cab barely tapped him, sending Booth onto its hood, but just for a moment, rolling off, heading onto the sidewalk, where startled pedestrians tumbled out of his way, like bowling pins going down in advance of an oncoming ball.

Then Booth veered back into the street, winding, weaving through traffic that was slowing for a light. Horrigan would see him, then not see him, and his gut was starting to ache, his breath starting to give way. He was winded. He was so fucking winded!

But the other agents hadn't caught up, and he saw Booth, not really getting a good look at him, but saw his prey, just as Booth rounded the corner on I Street and paused to catch his own breath, to look to see how near his pursuer was, and in that moment, Booth leaned his palm on the hood of a Ford Escort that had paused for the light.

Then Booth was gone.

Horrigan, hating himself, hating the over half a century this weary body of his had been alive, gasped for air, wondering if the paramedics would come for real this time. He stood in the street, a gun in hand, as if defying cars to hit him.

"Can't make it," he panted. "Can't fucking make it. . . ."

But the car Booth had touched, had laid his goddamn hand on, was coming right toward Horrigan. He stood straight, aimed the gun at the oncoming driver, whipped out his badge with his free hand and shouted, "Secret Service! Stop!"

The driver did so, screechingly, and, like a demented carhop, an exhausted Horrigan leaned against the side of the man's car, by the driver's window, and said, "I'm impounding your vehicle."

D'Andrea came running up.

"Booth put his hand on the hood of this car!" Horrigan shouted to his partner. "Keep everybody the fuck away from it!"

The driver, a round-faced guy in his thirties in a shirt and loosened tie, said, "Impounding my car? For five lousy parking tickets?"

Horrigan almost laughed at that, but resisted the urge, afraid he might cough up blood. He put his gun and badge away, bending, resting his hands on his knees, while uniformed agents surrounded the vehicle like the President's life depended on it.

Which Horrigan sincerely believed was the case.

12

● ●

Horrigan looked like a man from outer space, in the goggles; but through their amber lenses, as he and D'Andrea watched fingerprinting technicians work their laser-beam wonders on the hood of the impounded car in a Secret Service garage, he could see it, a heavenly vision. . . .

The glowing palm print, with five beautiful, near-perfect fingerprints, brought to life after red-orange powder had been brushed on, turning colors when bombarded by various bands of light.

The agent smiled.

"Perfect," Horrigan said.

That evening, in the computer center of the J. Edgar Hoover Building, an edifice as grim and squat as the man it was named for, an FBI technician sat before an amber computer screen in a room filled with many such screens and many such technicians. At this hour, however, only about a quarter of the desks were filled. The night shift lacked the day shift's frantic pace.

On the computer screen, blown up ten times, was a right-hand forefinger print, beneath the designation, "Fingerprint Sample #337-04B."

The technician, a young, sandy-haired, bespectacled wonk in a white shirt, black tie and no jacket, entered relevant information off a file card with efficiency but no particular enthusiasm. He had no idea what the print he was processing pertained to.

Allowing the computer to do its magic, he leaned back in his desk chair and returned to the dog-eared page of the paperback thriller he was reading, *Danger in D.C.* He tuned out the whirring of the machine as thousands of fingerprints were rapidly superimposed over the print, as the computer speed-searched for a match-up.

When after four minutes and a few seconds, such a match occurred, the technician, lost in his paperback, didn't notice at first; but soon the monitor began flashing the words "CLASSIFIED—NOTIFY C-12."

Its strobing caught his attention, and he sat up and studied the message, which confused him, as in over a year in this post, he'd never encountered any such message before.

He called out to his supervisor. "Hey, Chris! Something weird over here. You know what this means?"

His supervisor, a dark-haired, bespectacled, heavier, earlier-model wonk, hurried over. He stared at the screen and his face went pale. It was as if he were a doctor viewing his own terminal X rays.

"What's wrong?" the young tech asked.

"Nothing. Hit abort."

"Abort?"

"You heard me."

The tech shrugged, did as he was told, as the supervisor picked the file card off his desk and tore it into fourths and tossed it in a nearby wastebasket.

Outside, in the FBI waiting room, Horrigan paced like an expectant father. D'Andrea, leafing through a *People* magazine from six months ago, was reading an article about a pop star he'd completely forgotten about.

The dark-haired heavyset supervisor emerged from a doorway and sighed and shook his head.

"I'm sorry, Mr. Horrigan," he said, with a tight smile. "Afraid we came up empty."

Horrigan's eyes slitted. "Are you sure?"

The supervisor gestured expansively. "We ran the print against everything we've got . . . and we've *got* everything. I'm very sorry."

"Fuck," Horrigan said.

"As I said," the supervisor said, and shrugged, and was gone.

"What a lousy goddamn break," D'Andrea said, tossing his magazine aside.

Horrigan was already leaving. Hands dug in his pockets, shoulders slumped, he walked quickly down the corridor like a mean kid looking for a can to kick—or better still, a cat.

D'Andrea tagged along, having to work to keep up. "That rules out veterans, government employees, anybody with any kind of major criminal record. . . ."

"No kidding."

"So where does that leave us?"

"Up a certain creek where they don't give you a paddle."

D'Andrea shook his head. "I thought we had him."

"I did have him. I lost him." He slammed a fist into his hand. "I fucking lost him."

"Frank . . ."

Horrigan stopped and sighed. Lifted his head, looked around like a scout checking for Indians; but there was nothing to see but FBI corridor. "Tomorrow I leave with the President."

"God. Good luck."

"Afraid the President needs it more than I do."

"Shit. He'll be there, won't he? Booth."

"Yes he will."

"And you'll be there to stop him."

Horrigan twitched a scowl. "Yeah. Right. Anyway, you keep at it."

"At Booth, you mean?" D'Andrea's eyes bugged. "What the hell should I do?"

"How the hell should I know? You're a grown-up. They pay you to be a detective, don't they? Fucking detect."

Shaking his head hopelessly, D'Andrea opened the door and the night, which had turned cold, chilled them as they moved out into it.

Horrigan walked on ahead.

"Y'know, partner," D'Andrea called out, "you're a real pain in the ass when things don't go your way."

"It's not like you weren't warned," Horrigan said, and headed toward the nearest bus stop.

Leary looked like a man from outer space, in the protective goggles. It was the next day, in the workshop area of his dingy basement apartment. On a

· **106** ·

CD boom box nearby, the *Sgt. Pepper* album played at low volume.

He also wore an organic vapor mask, heavy splattered chemical apron and nitrile safety gloves. Sweat beading on his balding skull, lost in concentration, he sat at his workbench, combining two inert elements in a metal cylinder. It was dangerous work, creating toxic fumes, generating a lot of heat. But he knew what he was doing. The resin he was creating was, after all, his own formula.

The molds of the pieces of the gun were ready, lumpish plastic shells with intricate brownish yellow interiors, and he poured the mixture into the first one.

Under the vapor mask, he smiled.

"Perfect," he said.

13

●●●●●●●●●●●●●●●●●●●●●●●●

Horrigan, standing post in the corridor of the
Radisson Hotel in St. Paul, Minnesota, wondered
how many hours of his life he had spent enduring
such boredom. Weeks, surely—probably months,
maybe even a year or more, all told—spent in
deserted hotel corridors, waiting for the seconds
to pile into minutes, tediously amassing themselves
into hours. This was why agents burned out so
quickly on Presidential Protection duty: maintaining razor-sharp mental alertness and instantaneous
reaction time while suffering hours of boredom.

And those hours of boredom, as agent Dennis
McCarthy had once put it, were relieved only by
"moments of terror triggered by nothing more than
a car backfiring along a Presidential motorcade
route."

The last week had been a blur of numbing boredom
and frenzied activity, as the President hopscotched
through twelve Midwestern states in half as many
days. The press spoke of the President's campaign

staff's "desperate attempt to shore up their candidate's fortunes in the heartland" as the clock ticked on the final five weeks before the election.

And from that first morning at Andrews Air Force Base, when the President, his wife and advisors disembarked the Marine One helicopter en route to Air Force One, Frank Horrigan—as well as Lilly Raines—had formed part of the protective perimeter.

In Des Moines, Iowa, in a pounding rain, Horrigan—running alongside the Presidential limousine in the motorcade—slipped and fell on his ass in the middle of Fleur Drive; in Ames, at Iowa State, still aching from the fall, he stood along an auditorium wall during a rally where, onstage, the President spoke to a cheering contingency of solid middle Americans. But Horrigan wasn't listening to a speech he'd already heard half a dozen times, nor was he even looking at Lilly Raines, up onstage with the Man. He was studying faces in this corn-fed crowd of students, farmers, businessmen, housewives, wondering if one of them was a madman who nicknamed himself Booth.

The fabled Iowa countryside had been blotted out by rain, but the dreary flatness of Nebraska was all too evident in unseasonable heat that felt more like July than October. Keeping pace with the limo on the Omaha motorcade was an endurance test, though far preferable to the task, within a hangarlike exposition hall, of holding back hogs for the President's photo op with a group of farmers and their prize-winning porkers. Horrigan carried pig shit on his shoes into at least the next three states.

Because of the hopscotch nature of the swing,

Horrigan couldn't have reconstructed the order of events of the past week if his life depended on it. Had they done the Corn Palace in Mitchell, South Dakota, before or after the airport rally in Fargo, North Dakota? He could picture the President silhouetted against oil rigs, remembered it was Oklahoma City, but could that really have been the same day as the Gateway Arch rally in St. Louis? Who the hell knew, at this point?

It made him dizzy to consider the thousands of faces his eyes had surveyed, searching for a would-be assassin he'd seen only at a distance, and who had been in disguise at the time. But Horrigan felt—or anyway, hoped—that when he next locked eyes on Booth, he would *know* him.

Or was he just kidding himself? Booth could easily have been among the rowdy group of environmental protesters who had been waiting at the hotel today, to wave their placards and chant their angry slogans at the Chief Executive. Seemed the President wasn't doing enough about the Greenhouse Effect and global warming. After that sweltering October day in Omaha, Horrigan suspected the protesters might be right.

As Horrigan and the other agents had formed their phalanx about the President, steering him toward the Radisson Hotel's lobby entryway, a long-haired guy in a khaki jacket had lurched forward, past the police. Booth? Horrigan flipped a fist into the man's groin, and nodded to another agent, who quietly collared the guy before his howls had even died down.

But it hadn't been Booth. Not even a protester—just a voter who wanted to express his confidence in the President. Now, standing post in the Radisson corridor outside the Presidential suite, Horrigan smiled to himself, wondering if that vote might just have been lost.

A uniformed agent, with a German shepherd on a leash, passed by.

"Sniff out any bombs today, pooch?" Horrigan asked.

The dog gazed at him curiously, as if deciding whether or not to answer.

The disturbingly young-looking agent half-smiled and said, "No bombs. He's located some room-service leftovers, though."

"I bet." He scratched the dog behind its ears. "Save me a french fry, boy."

The agent and the dog continued on. Horrigan glanced at his watch. Not much longer. If the hotel bar could provide him with an inch or two of Jameson, and a piano to noodle at, he could be a complete person again.

The door to the Presidential Suite opened and Lilly slipped out. She wore another of the loose pants suits, this time with a green top, which she of course filled out admirably. She was wearing her reddish-blond hair down, and it brushed her shoulders.

She looked amazingly fresh, considering what the agents had been through these past six days.

"Agent Raines," he said.

"Agent Horrigan," she said.

"Did the First Lady ask about me?"

Lilly leaned against the wall, smirked cutely. "Why? Haven't you gotten to know them yet?"

"No."

"Why not?"

He shrugged. "Don't like to get close to the people I'm protecting."

"Ah. Don't want to get attached to them."

He gave her a wry smile. "Maybe I'm afraid I'll find out they're not worth taking a bullet for."

She smiled back, shook her head, her hair shimmering. "You're not half as hard as you make out to be, are you, Frank?"

His smile turned mock-innocent. "How hard would you like me to be?"

Her smile froze, and their eyes locked.

Footsteps on the carpeted hallway turned both their heads; a young agent was striding toward them, looking far too eager for this time of night.

"My replacement," Horrigan said. "A fetus with a badge and gun."

"They *are* looking younger and younger," Lilly admitted.

Soon Horrigan was a happy man—he had found a baby grand piano in the corner of the nearly deserted hotel lounge. Nobody protested when he sat down and began fluidly to play "I Didn't Know What Time It Was."

Lilly, leaning against the piano, looking very feminine and not at all like a cop, had a dreamy smile. She was impressed by his playing—he could tell. And he was glad. He was trying to impress her.

But he was also enjoying having his fingers on the keys again. Music was his best, his only, therapy, really. You couldn't think about your petty problems when you played. Work went away. Of course, music could speak to deeper problems, could stir memories, but somehow that was all right. Somehow that was necessary.

Then he missed a note, quickly recovered, raised an eyebrow at her. That's what he got, trying to impress a girl. Woman. Person.

"Ever play for a President?" she asked him.

"Hell, I've played *with* Presidents."

"Truman?"

"Hey, I'm not *that* fuckin' old."

Her laugh was easy, that rippling-water laugh he was coming to love. She sipped her glass of sherry. "Who, then?"

"Well . . . Nixon and I did a pretty mean 'Moonglow.'"

"I heard something about you and him."

"Oh?" He shifted into "The More I See You."

"I heard ol' Tricky Dick didn't think you smiled enough."

Horrigan laughed. "Not true, not true." He gave her a taste of his truly awful W. C. Fields impression: "A vicious rumor, my dear."

"What's the truth behind it?"

"Nixon and me, we got along swell—that lovable crook. It was that peckerhead chief of staff of his I butted heads with."

"Haldeman?"

"H. R. 'Bob' himself. Sargent reminds me of him, more than a little." He watched his fingers stroking the keys, and the memory rushed back, and he shared it with her. "One time, at a campaign rally in Boston, Haldeman told me to clear out some protesters. Didn't want the TV cameras to pick up on 'em. I refused."

"Refused?"

"Yeah. I pointed something out to him."

"What?"

"That it's a free country. I told him it had been in all the papers."

She laughed warmly. "I bet Bob was on your ass after that."

"All the time, all the time." He segued into "You'd Be So Nice to Come Home To."

"So it was *Haldeman* who complained that you didn't smile enough?"

"Bingo," he said. "One day he says to me, 'Agent *Horr*-igan'—he always emphasized the 'whore' sound, see—'I command you to smile more often.' God. 'Command,' yet. So I gave him the stare."

He demonstrated his stone-face scowl and she giggled, dipping her head, making the shimmery red-blond hair sway.

"Then he says, 'Mister, when I'm talking to you, I *am* the President.' And I said, 'The President? Why, you look more like a weasel in a bad suit to me, sir.'"

The laugh rippled. "Nice touch, that—the 'sir.' Very classy, Frank."

He smiled, lifted his eyebrows. "Next day they transferred me to the Foreign Dignitaries Protective Division. I wound up guarding Fidel Castro when he came to the U.N."

She winced. "Ouch," she said.

"Yeah ouch. One of our most hated enemies, and I'm supposed to take a bullet for the son of a bitch."

"Dirty job, but . . ."

"Know what? I found out, later, that the CIA was trying to knock Fidel off, at the time. Hell . . . why didn't they just ask me?"

She lifted her sherry. "Here's to bureaucracy."

He grinned, took his right hand away from the keys to lift his glass of Jameson and clink it with hers. Then he sipped the smooth Irish whiskey and played some more, working into "I've Grown Accustomed to Her Face," giving it a nice jazzy syncopation.

"Frank . . . how come you never wear sunglasses when you stand post? Even running alongside the limo, your eyes are naked to the sun."

"I admit the glare can be a problem," he said, "but then I'd lose *my* glare, and that's my secret weapon."

"Really?"

"Really. I like those goddamn wackos to be able to see the whites of my eyes. I want them to know they got to get past somebody meaner, and crazier, than they are."

He stopped playing, and turned on the full-wattage scowl.

"Whoa!" she said, rearing back. "That could curdle milk, boy!"

"Give it a try. You can do it."

"Okay," she said, shaking her head, hair shimmering, getting herself prepared. Then she leveled her own intense, angry gaze on him, before breaking down into laughter after a few seconds.

"Not bad," he said. "Not milk-curdling, but you're getting there. For the time being, though . . . I'd stick to the shades."

"Okay, okay . . . let me try again." She smoothed her hair, straightened her shoulders, cleared her throat, prepared herself mentally, and hit him with an icy, unblinking gaze. He shot it right back at her.

And then something happened.

The ice in those big brown eyes of hers turned to fire, first smoldering, then a full burn; her lips quivered, and he reached his face up to hers, about to kiss her when she turned away, as if ashamed.

He settled back down on the piano bench. "Why, Agent Raines—are you blushing?"

"Fuck you, Horrigan."

"I was hoping maybe that was the idea."

She tried to be mad, but started to laugh. "You're terrible."

"No. Horrible. Keep it straight. What exactly are you afraid of?"

She raised one eyebrow, pushed off the piano, standing. "Of . . . making a mistake. A big one. Good night, Frank."

She gathered her purse and walked away, slowly, across the nearly empty lounge.

Look back, baby, he thought. *Look back at me, now . . .*

She did. The briefest glance, a shy, uneasy glance. But it was all he needed.

He followed her across the lobby, where she nodded to an agent on duty there, and she was already on the elevator when he stepped on. He stood beside her, till the doors closed, then he faced her.

At first he thought her expression was anger, but then he knew it was something else, and pulled her to him; she made the slightest move to pull away, then her eyes half-closed and she might have been drunk when she said, "Oh, fuck it," but she wasn't drunk with anything but the heat of the moment, as his lips found hers and they clutched at each other in a desperate embrace.

Her mouth under his began to withdraw as she

tried to stop kissing and start speaking, an alarmed hum being the result; he backed off and saw her eyebrows raised high as she pointed with a finger like a gun to the floor indicator over the doors.

When those doors opened on the next floor, revealing agents Bill Watts and Matt Wilder waiting for a ride, discussing a computer printout as they did, Agent Raines stood at one side of the elevator, and Agent Horrigan at the other. Both were prim and bandbox proper, as they stepped out to greet their fellow agents.

"Bill," Horrigan said, cool but cordial. "Matt."

Ever sour, Watts handed Lilly the printout. "Updates on tomorrow."

"Thanks," she said, taking it. "Good night, gentlemen."

And she briskly walked off, down the hall, alone.

Wilder held the elevator open as Watts handed Horrigan a copy of the printout, before stepping aboard. Horrigan made sure they saw him heading down the hall, in the opposite direction from Lilly's room, before the elevator doors glided shut.

He didn't have to knock. She was waiting in her doorway for him. She locked and night-latched her door behind him, and switched off the light, and thrust herself into his arms for an even deeper, more volcanic kiss than their first one.

Soon the floor of Lilly's hotel room was a scattering of his and hers apparel and hardware—shoes, guns, handcuffs, earphones, wrist mikes, shirts, a pair of Kevlar bulletproof vests.

"Don't forget your extendible baton," he told her slyly.

"Don't forget yours," she said, with a nasty little

smile, and bit at his ear as he unbuckled his belt, unzipping, letting his trousers slide to the floor. She was down to her lingerie, and he took her in his arms, more gently than before but no less passionately, lowering her onto the bed, smothering her mouth with his; he was shocked and thrilled by her yearning, which seemed to match his own, and then she was under him, looking up at him tenderly, and he was feeling an emotion he thought had long since died when the fucking phone rang.

Her face tightened; a flash of sorrow and, what? Not shame, surely. . . .

He rolled off and let her slide over to the phone, and she sat on the edge of the bed, with her back to him, as she answered it.

"Raines," she said, coolly professional. She listened for a while. Nodded. Nodded again. "Sure. Be right down."

She put the receiver back in the hook, and without turning to look at him, said, "Traveller is losing ground in Wisconsin. Two last-minute events have been added for Milwaukee, tomorrow morning."

"Lilly . . ."

"Watts wants to see me. Now."

He reached over, touching her shoulder, gently, but she pulled away, getting up, walking with her back to him, leaning down, struggling to quickly pick up her littered clothing and Secret Service gear. She had a little trouble, sorting out her things from his, and a few items dropped to the floor from the bundle in her arms, making her awkward walk to the bathroom even more so.

She didn't look at him once.

But she did stop to say, "Frank . . . this isn't right.

It's just too damn complicated. I'm sorry."

She shut herself in the bathroom and Horrigan sat up in bed, propped a pillow behind him and put his hands behind his head, elbows winged out. He smiled ruefully to himself, shook his head, murmured, "Complicated, Lilly, yes—but well worth it."

He glanced toward the closed bathroom door, got out of bed and dressed, reassembling himself. Then he noticed something.

She'd inadvertently switched one item for his, and it made his rueful smile turn into a grin. He'd have to wait for just the right moment to point out her mistake.

She had taken *his* extendible baton.

14

....

Leary had been in his rat-hole basement apartment, away from the workshop area, sitting in his thrift-shop easy chair, watching his portable TV on its VCR stand, eating microwave-warmed spaghetti with a spoon from a single-serving can, when the KCOP newswoman announced the twelve-state campaign swing.

The black newswoman had been standing near the runway at Andrews Air Force Base, talking over the blare of a military brass band's stirring march.

"The President's campaign staff is hopeful," she almost shouted, "that when the swing concludes at a large rally at McCormick Center in Chicago, polls will confirm the President has won back his following among Midwestern voters."

It excited Leary, when he saw Frank Horrigan among the agents and aides following the President onto Air Force One; he thought, *I know him! I know that guy!* It made him feel part of this moment in history—oh, such a good, even *exhilarating* feeling—

but it felt even better knowing how much *bigger* a part he was *going* to be. . . .

Immediately, he called a travel service and booked an open-ended ticket to Los Angeles—"I may be making some Midwestern stops on my return," he told the agent. When? Next available flight, of course.

Going through the metal detector at Dulles, wearing a sweat suit and Dodgers cap, he set off the alarm. Smiling placidly at the attendant, he removed his lucky rabbit's-foot key chain, and tried again. No problem this time, and his good-luck charm and keys were returned to him.

In Los Angeles, Leary checked into a cheap motel near the airport and assumed his James Carney persona—glasses, business suit, briefcase. In a rental Buick, he drove through downtown Los Angeles to a rundown, mostly Hispanic neighborhood where he pulled up before a decrepit office building.

Footsteps echoing down the marble hall, wood-and-pebbled-glass office doors on either side of him, Leary stopped at a door inscribed "MICROSPAN CORPORATION." Humming his Beatles tune, he got out his rabbit's foot and used a key, stepping inside, almost tripping over an accumulation of junk mail that had dropped through the door slot.

The modest-size office looked larger than it was because it was barren of anything but a single beat-up desk and a wooden chair. Light filtered in around drawn, patched shades. He didn't bother switching on the overhead light—he knew it was burned out.

Locking the door behind him, Leary bent to gather the mail and carried it over gleefully, like a child expecting a mail-order toy, and tossed the pile on the desk. He sat and sorted through it, smiling when he came to the small brown cardboard box post-marked Santa Monica.

Southwest Bank.

He opened the box and found his Microspan corporate checks.

"Thank you, Pam," he said softly. "You were efficient right to the end."

He sat, humming, tore the first check from its crisp, fresh pad and filled it out in the amount of $50,000—payable to "The California Victory Fund." With a smug kiss of a smile, he removed an envelope from his briefcase (the desk was empty) and addressed it the same way. A typed letter on Microspan Corporate stationery was already tucked into the envelope, prepared back home. He licked it shut.

At Los Angeles International Airport, carry-on bag in hand, he walked along briskly, wearing the sweat suit again, but now the Dodgers cap had been replaced with a Milwaukee Brewers one. Whistling, he dropped the envelope into a mail slot and headed for the airport gate.

Once again, his lucky rabbit's-foot key ring set off the metal detector, and he smiled and shrugged at the bored attendant, dropping the keys into the tray he was provided.

How he relished it every time that lucky piece was handed back to him. It made him just want to laugh out loud.

But he didn't.

The next day, in Milwaukee, in a hard, driving rain, Leary stood beneath an umbrella, his Brewers cap snugly on, worn the correct way, bill out, none of that backward rapper crap for him. He was no disrespectful monkey. Despite the weather, the crowd outside the convention hall was sizable, and Leary wasn't the only person wearing a Brewers cap, not hardly.

The police held them back, but he was only fifty feet away from where Horrigan stood, without an umbrella, getting drenched, finger against his earpiece, frowning, listening, waiting for the Presidential limo to arrive.

"Poor baby," Leary said to himself quietly.

When the limo pulled in, and the President stepped out, chaos seemed to reign—the enthusiastic crowd shouting over the driving downfall.

"Mr. President!"

"Over here, Mr. President!"

"Hey, Mr. President, look over here!"

The media was swarming on the beaming, waving politician, flash cameras popping like mini-bursts of lightning, TV cameramen with portables on their shoulders angling for a shot, as the Secret Service agents rode herd on both the President himself and the press.

Leary had to hand it to Horrigan and his fellow agents. They were maintaining their cool, efficient, professional duty, in the face of daunting circumstances.

He felt a rush of warmth, despite the cold rain. He truly admired Horrigan.

The affection he felt for the agent, standing so near him, was almost overwhelming; it was, deep within Leary, matched only by similar feelings of contempt and hatred.

Horrigan, one of the agents circling the on-the-move President, was searching the crowd with his eyes, now. Leary kept his face impassive, but inside he was jumping like a child who had to wee wee: a moment of truth was coming, and the anticipation was terrible and wonderful. . . .

Leary could almost feel Horrigan's eyes as they fixed upon his face, like probing lasers.

And traveled right across to the next face, and the next.

Then the President—and Agent Horrigan, and the rest of the agents, not that Leary cared about *them*—were inside the Convention Hall.

Leary, under his umbrella, walked away from a crowd that wasn't yet dispersing. A solitary figure, he was happy with himself. He, too, had maintained his cool. But he was also thinking about Horrigan's rain-streaming face as the agent's hard, angry eyes had slowly scanned the crowd.

The streaming droplets almost made it look as if Horrigan were weeping.

Poor baby, Leary thought again. *You'll soon enough have reason to.*

15

....

Horrigan felt like shit.

His head was burning, his nose running, his muscles aching, and as the Boeing 747 (known as Air
Force One when the President was aboard—which
he currently was) lurched through a rain-wracked,
lightning-rent sky, Horrigan was keeping an eye
on the air sickness bag in the pocket of the First
Class–type seat in front of him.

Across the aisle from him in the darkened cabin, Matt Wilder and several other agents slept;
many seats were empty: elsewhere in the plane, in
the Secret Service communications center, things
would still be hopping as Bill Watts undertook last-
minute security measures for Chicago; and in Chief
of Staff Harry Sargent's spacious cabin, a Presidential speech was no doubt being written and
rewritten, with the likely result something they'd
all heard before, *ad nauseam*. . . .

That was a word he wished hadn't occurred to him,

his stomach, like the plane, pitching and rolling. He had resisted taking any more of the cold medicine because it made him drowsy, and he wanted to read the report D'Andrea had faxed him, before shutting off the little reading light and giving in to the stuff.

But intermittent lightning bolts of migraine were defeating him. He reached for the bottle of medicine in the seat pocket in front of him; then he would ring for an Air Force steward up in the forward galley, to get him some coffee or water or something to wash it down. . . .

Only he couldn't get the goddamn bottle open. He wrestled with it, sweating, too sick to know how foolish he looked.

Trying not to spill her cup of coffee, Lilly Raines—looking a little white around the gills herself, reddish-blond hair swinging as the plane was buffeted—braced herself against the seats on this side of the wide aisle, and that one, as she moved haltingly, awkwardly, toward Horrigan.

Her smile was wry but not unsympathetic as she settled into the seat next to him, lowering the tray in front of her for her coffee cup.

"You know why you can't open that, don't you?" she asked him, watching him struggle with the cold medicine bottle.

"No. Why?" He was gritting his teeth. *Fucking thing!*

"It's childproof."

That made him laugh, a little.

"Here—give it to me," she said, and he did, and she took it, popped it open, shook out a capsule, loaned him her coffee.

"Thanks," he said, swallowing the pill with a gulp of the hot black liquid.

She arched an eyebrow. "You look like something the cat dragged in."

"Thanks for sharing," he said.

Thunder boomed, the rain-streaked window next to him strobing white with lightning.

"Under the weather, huh?" she asked.

"I wish we were."

"Huh?"

"Under this weather."

The plane rocked with the turbulence; his stomach dropped a couple thousand feet, no parachute. He hoped he could keep the goddamn pill down.

She reached for his lap, he raised an eyebrow and she smirked, saying, "Don't get any ideas," as she lifted off the manila folder marked "Alias John Wilkes Booth."

As she thumbed through the faxed contents, he asked, "Traveller getting some sleep?"

She nodded, scanning the pages.

"What's the ETA?" he asked.

"Few minutes. Eleven-forty-something."

"Watts on top of everything?"

She nodded again. "I just reported in to him. We've got the motorcade route secured. Chicago police snipers already in position. Agents at the hotel."

"Good. And the Watch List?"

"Twenty-three regional crazies under surveillance. Chicago Police Intelligence is helping out."

"What's the nearest hospital?"

"St. Anne's. Extra units of Traveller's blood type on hand. Accessible to the alternate route as well."

"That's good. Watts is doing good."

She glanced up from the file. "I thought you considered our fearless leader a 'prick.'"

"I didn't say he wasn't a prick. I said he was doing a good job."

"This psychological profile," she said, waving the slender "Booth" file, "makes for pretty light reading."

He sneered. "Crack team of Secret Service psychologists analyze his voice, his behavioral patterns and come up with the brilliant conclusion that Booth '*may* intend' to harm the President."

She shrugged. "Experts," she said mildly derisive.

"So," he asked gently, "did you make a big mistake?"

That caught her off guard. "Huh?"

"In the bar the other night . . . you said you were afraid of making a big mistake. Did you?"

She winced, embarrassed. "Horrigan, nothing really happened . . ."

"Something almost happened, you mean. To me, the 'big mistake' is that it didn't."

"Horrigan . . ."

"Frank."

"Frank." She was searching; she seemed almost in pain. "It's not like we work for a brokerage house or an ad agency or something. . . . This job we do, it's . . . Fraternization is just . . ."

"Fraternization?" he asked in a mild, amused voice, but he really was irritated, and a little hurt. "Is 'fraternize' what we were about to do?"

She shook her head, gently; hair swaying with the rocking of the plane. "Let's be realistic."

He narrowed his eyes, gave her an appraising stare.

"Let me see how my deductive abilities stack up, in my feverish condition. . . . You had a relationship with an agent, once upon a time—and it turned out bad."

"No." Embarrassed but not angry, she even laughed softly and said, "That was the problem. He *wasn't* an agent."

"Ah. A civilian. He wanted you to quit your dangerous job for him and get barefoot and pregnant—like a good girl."

"Something like that."

"So he left you. Broke your heart."

The brown eyes registered pain. "Actually . . . I left him."

"Oh?"

Her smile was self-mocking; she rolled her eyes. "I left him, 'cause I refused to quit my job over him." She sighed. "You are a goddamn detective, Horrigan."

"I know people. It's . . ."

"What they pay you for, right." She swallowed, looked at nothing, looked into herself and her past. "It *did* break my heart. I was . . . in the St. Louis Field Office. He seemed to be accepting what I did, all right . . ."

"What was he?"

"An insurance agent."

"No comment."

She smirked again, said, "I thought I loved him. Maybe I did, maybe I didn't. But a month after he gave me the engagement ring, I got transferred. To the Protective Division."

"In Washington. And he didn't want to follow you."

"He didn't want to follow me. He wanted me to quit my job and stay behind."

A half-smile twitched in his cheek. "If you were a *man* who got transferred, and he were a woman, he'd have followed *you*."

"You finally did it, Frank."

"What?"

"Came up with that appropriate sexist remark."

They smiled at each other; it was warm. Not volcanic, but Horrigan would settle for warm, for now.

"You *couldn't* leave the service," Horrigan said, mildly teasing.

"Why not?"

"They'd have made you turn in your gun."

Her laugh was sudden as his insight blindsided her. "Isn't it crazy? I love this fucking job. The pressure, the adrenaline rush . . . knowing history's right next to me, being made. Sounds hokey, huh?"

"No," he said, softly, meaning it. "Not at all."

She leaned back in the seat, her eyes traveling to the darkness above. "You know, when I take a vacation, my life feels like it's . . . going in slow motion. I just can't *stand* it."

"So that's why."

"Why what?"

"Why I'm classified a potential 'big mistake.' " He was matter of fact, nothing negative in his tone. Almost clinically, he stated, "You swore you'd never again let a man come between you and the thing you love. And the thing you love is your career."

"Actually, Frank," she said, a little surprised, "that's very well put. In this line of work, how can either of us risk a relationship? I can't afford to think about how much my damn *feet* hurt, let alone—"

"But your career isn't all you love."

"What do you mean?"

His tone was mischievous as he said, "Well, it's obvious—you love me, too. And it scares you."

She looked at him with a glazed smile and then slowly shook her head and let her laugh ripple; thunder punctuated it.

"I don't know that I'd call it love, exactly, Frank . . . animal magnetism maybe. Affection . . . no question about it. But love?"

"I'd quit my job for you."

Her eyes popped; he might have hit her with a plank.

"You'd what?"

"Quit my job for you."

Her composure back, she gave him another smirk, clearly not believing him for a second. "And why in hell would you do that?"

He looked out the rain-streaked window into darkness. "Maybe I swore I'd never again let my career come between me and a woman."

Her mouth smiled, but her forehead frowned.

As if to demonstrate how futile their relationship would be, Watts's voice on a nearby overhead speaker squawked, *"Ten minutes to touchdown in Chicago."*

"You know, Frank," she said, touching his arm, changing the subject and her tone, "you really do look sick."

"That's because I am sick."

"Then I think you should consider letting Watts

replace you, tomorrow, with somebody from the Chicago Field Office. Just till you shake this flu bug."

"Bullshit. Nobody qualified."

"Don't be silly. There's probably half a dozen veterans of the PPD in the Chicago office. Now, be realistic—you're going to be standing post, either feverish, or doped up, and either way, you can't do your job effectively."

He bristled. "I'm more effective in my goddamn sleep than half the agents on this detail."

"What a touching display of camaraderie. I think you should simply tell Watts you're sick . . ."

He rolled his eyes. "Oh, how he'd love that! The old man can't keep up the pace. Look, Lil—I have to be there, at the President's side. I have no fucking choice."

"Why, in heaven's name?"

"It's personal. Let's leave it at that."

"Personal between you and Watts, you mean?"

"No!" He shook his head, frustrated. "No. Somehow, in some way sicker even than *I* am on this roller coaster of an airplane . . . somehow this is between me and Booth. I *have* to be there." His eyes narrowed. "I'm the only one he might tip himself to."

She drew in breath as if to speak, but as the lightning flashed again, throwing cold white across his face, she thought against it.

Then he said to her, warningly but warmly, "You just worry about you. Keep alert. *Don't* think about how much your feet hurt. It's going to be a big crowd. Be careful."

She nodded. Quietly she said, "Frank."

"Yeah?"

"Thanks for sharing," she said sincerely.

Then, smiling tightly, she patted his arm, got up, and left the cabin.

16

The rain came at an angle, with some Chicago wind behind it, threatening to knock Horrigan over. Or maybe he was just that weak, his eyes hot with fever, his face cold with rain; water streamed from his plastered-down hair into his eyes and mouth. Nasty fucking weather. . . .

He was standing outside the entrance of McCormick Center where a crowd's enthusiasm was getting literally dampened as they pushed and pressed, trying to get into the lobby's doors and out of the driving rain. Their progress was slowed by the metal detectors each person had to pass through upon entering. Tempers were running short, and attitudes seemed surly, even for Chicago.

Across the heads of these increasingly disgruntled constituents, Horrigan saw Wilder, getting similarly soaked. Speaking into the wrist mike clipped to his cuff, Horrigan said, "Way too wet for a photo op! Take Traveller underground."

Wilder nodded, and moved off to pass the information along—the motorcade, approaching down Lake Shore Drive, would opt for the underground entrance, due to Horrigan's judgment call. The continuing bad weather would completely fuck up media response; they might as well have stayed out by O'Hare Airport, and used the Rosemont Horizon.

Horrigan was pushing through the wet, unruly crowd, on his way inside, when he spotted another group of environmental protesters, their enthusiasm undaunted by the downpour, even though their placards were getting drenched, ink running, messages smearing.

Near the protesters, not pushing as hard to get in as most of the crowd, stood a man in a dark raincoat, dark glasses and fedora. The guy looked like a 1930s political cartoonist's idea of an anarchist. . . .

Booth? he wondered.

Horrigan's fever-ridden brain, bubbling like boiling water, seized upon the possibility obsessively, and he pressed desperately through the crowd. He knew not to shout "Secret Service"—the last thing they needed was panic in this potential mob, and all he'd had was a glimpse of dark glasses and a fedora. . . .

As he neared the protesters, a placard—accidentally, but no less threateningly—swung toward his head, and he ducked, and tumbled to the slick sidewalk, and when he worked his way back up, he couldn't spot the guy in the crowd, anymore. He craned his neck, desperately searching the sea of bobbing heads for the fedora, but it was gone.

The rain began hammering down even harder. He wiped the dampness away with the harsh sleeve of his trench coat, but he couldn't wipe away his apprehension.

Nor could he wipe away the notion, the feeling, the certainty that was burning in his gut.

Booth was here.

Walking briskly down a corridor past uniformed agents walking their bomb-sniffing hounds, Horrigan ducked in a rest room to dry off. Even so, his hair was still damp, clinging to his scalp, and—after a glance in the bathroom mirror—he knew it made him look half-crazed; but he couldn't help it. He had to get backstage.

There he found the President, his wife at his one side, Watts on the other, as the Chief Executive went over notes for the speech with that unpleasant bulldog chief of staff of his, Harry Sargent. They were loosely ringed by special agents, including Lilly and Matt Wilder. Filling the air was the muffled but almost deafening amplified voice of some local political bigwig, making an introduction out onstage.

Watts, noticing Horrigan's arrival, frowned and broke away from the President's inner circle, and walked quickly over to him. Lilly, eyes narrowing with worry, followed along, a step behind.

"You're late, Horrigan," Watts said brusquely.

I am the show, he thought, but said nothing.

"Your floor position is stage right," Watts added.

"I need a second with you," Horrigan said.

"That's all I can spare."

"I . . . I think Booth is here."

Watts sprang to attention, eyes flared. "You saw him? Well enough to *make* him? I thought, when you chased him, you didn't get a good enough look to make an I.D.!"

"I didn't. . . . I can't. But I think he's here."

"You *think*?"

"Call it a hunch."

"That's not what *I* call it." Watts's sigh was heavy, long, and sarcastic. "With all due respect to your several centuries of experience, as well as your no-doubt impressive psychic powers, we have seventy-five agents, two hundred Chicago cops and a bulletproof podium out there."

Horrigan, eyes hot, swallowed. "I just know he's here, that's all."

"If you don't mind," Watts said acidly, obnoxiously, "I think we'll just stick to the *existing* game plan."

The officious prick strode back to the President, while Lilly stayed behind. She looked at Horrigan with an ashen, concerned expression.

"Is that rain, or sweat on your forehead?" she asked.

He found a handkerchief in a pocket and mopped his brow. "Does it matter?"

"Yes it matters." She pressed her cool palm to his blazing head. "You're burning up! Frank . . ."

"*People!*" Watts shouted.

The other agents began filing out onstage. Lilly's mouth was poised to speak, her eyes huge with doubt.

He touched her arm; squeezed it. "Stay alert out there."

Soon Horrigan was in position down in front of the stage, as were a number of other agents. Still more agents were along the walls, all around the hall's perimeter. According to Watts, this constituted a more than sufficient number of agents for the task at hand—but, Horrigan knew, such a relative handful compared to the countless civilian bodies packing this house.

They were dried off now, these audience members, their enthusiasm extending even to the dull pronouncements of the local politico's speech which droned on from the podium; they willingly filled his pregnant pauses with the expected cheers and applause.

Finally an offstage voice boomed, *"Ladies and gentlemen—the President of the United States."*

And a brass band—or that is, a tape of a brass band on the sound system—blared "Hail to the Chief."

Carter wouldn't let them play that, Horrigan's fevered brain pointlessly reminded him. *Too pompous for a man of the people. . . .*

The crowd shot to its feet, cheering, whistling, stomping; the sound was overwhelming, the ovation mingling with the brass band into a cacophonous din. Horrigan's head pounded; eyes burned. . . .

Cameras began to flash and pop and flash and pop, like the thunder and lightning back on the plane, disorienting him, and a high spotlight, suddenly swinging down to catch the President as he strode out on the stage with the First Lady, almost blinded Horrigan. He looked away, momentarily, black spots blotting sections of his vision.

The President and First Lady had taken their places at the podium; behind them, Harry Sargent and agents Watts, Wilder and Raines took their positions.

The crowd's frenzied standing ovation continued,

and Horrigan forced his eyes to focus, blinking past the flashbulbs to study faces.

That smiling young guy in the Cubs T-shirt, is that a gun in his hand?

No.

A camera. Just a camera.

Why isn't that fat, sullen woman cheering? What the hell's she doing at a rally if she isn't a supporter of the President's?

The faces swam and blurred, each one looking more and more grotesque to him; even the happy faces seemed *wrong*, seemed to harbor violence. Hands waved balloons, red, white and blue, like disembodied bizarre heads, bobbing, weaving, now and then breaking free and floating. *Where are you, Booth?*

What's that skinny woman doing reaching into her purse? She looks pissed off!

A tissue. Just blowing her nose. . . .

Up by the spotlight, *is that a rifle barrel?*

No. Shotgun mike. Just a shotgun mike. . . .

But what is that guy next to him doing? That is a camera, isn't it?

Yes. A camera. . . .

Horrigan blinked, swallowed, composing himself, and then heard the sharp *pop*.

The gunshot sound sent him leaping onto the stage. Hitting his knees as he did, he rolled, scrambled to his feet, gun in hand, ignoring the pain, as the agents onstage—Watts, Lilly, Wilder and others—swarmed around the terrified President and First Lady, providing human shields.

The cheering in the vast hall had stopped, replaced by a collective gasp.

Eyes wild, a panicked Harry Sargent was down on his hands and knees, the bulldog on all fours, crawling behind the agents sheltering the President, getting back of that bulletproof podium.

Horrigan stood center stage, with the podium to his back, the gun in his hand, facing the crowd, the sweat trailing down his face like hot rain. He glared at the now dead silent, frozen gathering—it was *him* against *them*—gave them the full-wattage stare, searching, searching, searching every fucking face—*shoot again, Booth, you shoot again and we'll have your ass.* . . .

A red balloon, trailing toward the ceiling, popped. Horrigan flinched.

But recognized the sound, and knew at once the mistake he'd made.

As did everyone else onstage.

He glanced back at the President, but saw instead Bill Watts glaring at him contemptuously. Horrigan gave him an almost imperceptible shrug, before speaking into his cuff-mike: "All clear."

Before he climbed back off the stage, Horrigan caught a glimpse of Sargent—his sweat-streaked face purple with rage, his eyes narrow with embarrassment—scowling at him. An adversary had just turned into an enemy.

Some of the others were just sighing with relief, as the cordon of agents relaxed around the President, moving back into their assigned positions, as the President—making a graceful recovery from this awkward moment—slipped an arm around the First Lady's shoulder and waved enthusiastically at the crowd, both of them having the presence of mind to bestow beaming smiles on the assemblage.

The crowd, still on its feet, went crazy again, the cheers even wilder now, more impassioned, the whistles deafening.

But Horrigan couldn't hear any of it. He could hear only his own heart beating. He had seen, but turned quickly away from, Lilly's concerned, even pitying, gaze. He could feel how fully shaken he was.

What he now could not hear, see or feel was the presence of Mitch Leary—"Booth"—who sat far back in the crowd, a bland little smile tickling his lips, in no disguise save for a Sox cap (certainly not a fedora and sunglasses), watching the show through his binoculars, taking in Horrigan's inglorious moment, soaking up Horrigan's confusion and discomfort.

"Poor baby," Leary said.

But in the midst of cheers, no one heard him.

17
●●●●●●●●●●●●●●●●●●●●●●●●

A few hours later, at the Drake Hotel in Chicago, the Secret Service communications center was in the process of being turned back into a hotel room, as various agents—baby-faced young ones, Horrigan noted—dismantled the portable setup, tearing down and loading up the gear in padded, hard-shell flight cases.

In the midst of this orderly, routine chaos, Horrigan sat in an easy chair, uneasily awaiting the new asshole he was about to be torn.

A coldly furious Watts—agents Matt Wilder and Lilly Raines looking woeful on the sidelines—had just informed Horrigan that White House Chief of Staff Harry Sargent was on his way up.

"Be respectful," Watts ordered, shaking his finger. "Understand?"

Horrigan felt miserable; you could've fried an egg on his forehead, as long as you didn't ask him to eat it. "I'm not ten years old," he managed.

"Try to keep that in mind," Watts snapped.

Sargent barreled in, his tie flapping. He didn't stand on the ceremony of a greeting; he bulled over to where Horrigan sat and started right in.

"Do you have even the slightest idea how many goddamn votes you cost us today?"

"No."

Sargent threw up his hands, while the flu-ridden Horrigan just tried not to throw up.

"The President came off like a damn *coward* today," Sargent raved, "and on national TV!"

"I thought the President did all right."

"You did, did you?"

"Better than some."

Sargent leaned in; his eyes were bloodshot and the bags under them were black. He looked like Horrigan felt.

"What exactly do you mean by that, Agent Horrigan?"

"What do I mean by that?"

Lilly winced, touched her fingers to her forehead.

"Well," Horrigan said, "I mean that you're the one who came off looking like a fucking coward. Sir."

Sargent paced the area near Horrigan's chair, like a lion about to pounce; he sneered, snarled, "You think you're cute, Horrigan? You think you're tough? You think this is some kind of goddamn joke?"

"No. I think you're some kind of goddamn joke." Horrigan stood up, went head-to-head with the bastard—close enough, Horrigan hoped, to give Sargent the flu. "You're a joke because you don't have the slightest goddamn idea about what we have to do to keep your boss alive."

· 146 ·

As the two men stood inches apart, Horrigan gave him the full-wattage scowl and Sargent's nasty expression softened just around the edges; the coward in him was peeking out, just barely.

Watts interceded, pulling Horrigan back. "That's enough. Enough! Understood?"

Sargent shot Watts a withering look. "You keep this lunatic away from the President, *and* away from the White House."

And he pointed a thick finger at Horrigan, who was still giving him the stare. "And you sure as hell better keep him away from *me!*"

Half-delirious with fever, Horrigan laughed, but it sounded more like a cough. "Try to imagine how much you frighten me, Harry."

Close to losing it, Sargent waggled his scolding finger. "Call me Harry again, and you'll be chasing counterfeiters on a bobsled in Bum Fuck, Alaska."

Steaming, Sargent stormed out, nearly bumping into a young agent carting communications gear.

"Are you crazy?" Watts demanded, incredulous. "You can't talk to the White House chief of staff like that!"

"I don't work for him."

"No—you work for me. Or I should say, you *used* to work for me. You're off the detail." He checked his watch. To everyone, he said, "Downstairs for departure in two minutes."

Watts, followed by the rest of the gear-bearing young agents, stalked out. Matt Wilder sighed. Lilly stood with her arms folded, staring at the floor.

Horrigan, every bone, every muscle aching, flopped back in the easy chair.

"Here you go," Matt said, standing in front of

Horrigan, handing him a twenty spot.

"What's this for?" Horrigan asked, barely able to focus on the bill.

"About time I settled up that Super Bowl debt I owe you." Matt smiled warmly, patted him on the shoulder. "I don't care what anybody says or thinks—it was good to work with you again. Take it easy, pal."

Horrigan twitched a smile, nodded.

Then Matt was gone and it was just Horrigan and Lilly now, in a big empty hotel room.

She stood before him, head tilted to one side, gazing down at him with a bemused mixture of affection and irritation.

"You know," she said, "if you could have just been a little more gracious about it . . ."

"Not my strong suit."

"All you would have had to do was acknowledge that it was an unfortunate—"

He cut her off abruptly; even sharply. "I was just doing my job. I don't *apologize* for doing my job."

That hurt her; he could see it in her eyes, but he couldn't take back the words, and he wasn't sure he wanted to.

She said, "I didn't say you should apologize. But the President *was* humiliated. . . ."

"He's still alive, isn't he?"

"But we're here to safeguard his *dignity,* too."

"Where's that written? I don't give a damn about his dignity. It's his ass I'm hired to save."

Her eyes crinkled with faint amusement. "What about the time one of Jack Kennedy's girlfriends got caught after hours in the White House—and you said she was *your* plaything?"

· **148** ·

He looked away. "You believe every rumor you hear?"

"Some have the ring of truth. Frank—your pal Matt told me the whole story. How you got suspended without pay for a month? I'd say you were safeguarding *that* President's dignity."

"That was different."

"Different, how?"

"He was my friend. *He* was different."

Her smirk wasn't at all nasty. "Maybe *you* were different, then."

"Weren't we all? Wasn't the whole goddamn country?" His head swam with the fever; he felt like he might pass out at any moment. "Maybe I am a paranoid 'lunatic,' now—but thirty years or so ago, if I'd been paranoid like that, maybe he wouldn't be dead today. Maybe . . . maybe this country would be different, . . ."

He didn't know what he was saying.

"We're going to be late," she said.

I am the show.

"Go on," he said. "I need a second."

She nodded, her disappointment in him apparent, and went out. He covered his face with his hands for a moment, then got himself to his feet, stumbled into the bathroom, threw up in the commode, stood at the sink, splashed water on his face, dried himself off and went down to the lobby to take one last ride on Air Force One.

18
●●●●●●●●●●●●●●●●●●●●●●●●

A hundred years later, that evening, Horrigan was back in Washington, in his cluttered apartment, dropping four Alka-Seltzers into a glass of water. His fever had broken on the plane, but the headache and fatigue lingered.

He'd been greeted by a sympathetic Sam Campagna at Andrews Air Force Base, when Air Force One landed, and was given an impromptu invitation to dinner. Sam's wife, Louise, one of the sweetest human beings on the planet, had made room for him at the table in their fashionably appointed home in the Virginia suburbs.

After dinner, over drinks in the study, his longtime boss, his longtime friend, had suggested Horrigan retire. Live off his pension. His overhead was low, wasn't it? After all, these days he didn't spend money on anything but jazz records. Or was it CDs now?

"I want to stay on the Booth case," Horrigan had said.

"All right," Campagna reluctantly replied. "But as for the Protective Division, you gotta understand, there's nothing even I can—"

"I know."

They sat in silence. Campagna sipped his bourbon, Horrigan his Irish whiskey.

"Chicago was a first for me," Horrigan said. "I never been on the wrong side of a judgment call before. Unless you count Dallas. . . ."

"Nobody counts Dallas but you." Campagna's smile was both weary and understanding. "I hear in Chicago you had a fever of 103. That's been known to impair a man's judgment, for Christ's sake. And, hell—face it, Frank—you're getting too old for this shit."

When Campagna dropped him off, Horrigan had stopped by the neighborhood bar, to fool around on the piano, but it didn't help. He played "What a Difference a Day Made" for a while, but he just wasn't in the mood for irony. Or jazz. Or even whiskey.

Alka-Seltzer was his drink tonight. And good ol' rock 'n' roll. British Invasion. He tore the plastic from the *Sgt. Pepper* CD he'd bought; he removed Miles Davis, and popped in the Beatles. He programmed the CD player to play track 2, "With a Little Help from My Friends," ten times.

He was in his reclining chair, the empty Alka-Seltzer glass next to him, listening to that track for the sixth time, when the phone rang.

He turned down the stereo with his remote control and lifted the receiver from the hook, slowly.

"Hello?" he said, knowing who it would be.

The whispery voice was almost soothing: "What happened in Chicago, Frank?"

"Hello, Booth."

"You panicked."

"You were there, weren't you?"

"You know I was. You didn't see me . . . but you knew." A soft chuckle. "We're connected, you and I. . . . It's really . . . comforting, in a way, isn't it?"

"Not exactly."

Booth continued: "You know, sitting there, watching you, watching the President, I couldn't help thinking, after how that cowardly chickenshit behaved . . . *how* could you, why *would* you, risk your life to save a weakling like that? A strong man like you, Frank."

"What were you doing in Chicago, Booth?"

"Research."

"I see. Tell me, Booth. Why would a man like you risk his life to try to kill a 'weakling' like that?"

"Not 'try' to, Frank. I *will* kill him. And not *risk* it. You and I both know the odds: I'll *give* it. I'll give my life, and anyway, don't you have a psychological profile worked up on me yet, Frank? You're not slipping, are you?"

"I don't put much stock in that shit."

"Don't blame you. Me, either. A man's actions don't necessarily equal the sum of his psychological parts. It just doesn't work that way."

"How does it work?"

Booth's laugh was anything but "comforting."

He said, "Why, it *doesn't* work, Frank—you know that. It doesn't work at all, doesn't begin to. Does God punish the wicked, and reward the righteous? Of course not."

"Is that right?"

" 'Right' has nothing to do with it. Some people die because they do bad things. Some people die because they do good things. Others die simply because they're from Minneapolis. One nation under God, indivisible, with liberty and justice for all? Not hardly. False advertising, says me."

"If none of it means anything, Booth—then why bother killing the President?"

"To make a mark, Frank. To leave something behind. And, well . . . just to punctuate this dreary existence of ours."

"You need to get seriously laid."

"Maybe we have that in common, too."

"What else do we have in common, Booth?"

The voice sounded almost cozy. "I've seen the way you live . . . watched you alone in that bar, playing your piano, drinking your whiskey. . . . You feel empty inside, Frank, don't you? The good battles, they're over, they're gone. No great causes left to die for. Nothing left but . . . the game itself."

"The game?"

"Sure. That's why fate brought us together. Worthy opponents jousting on the field of irony. You on defense—me on offense."

"When's this game scheduled, Booth?"

"Why, it's happening now. Every minute of every day, Frank, till the clock winds down—or sudden death overtime."

Silence—except, faintly, for Ringo Starr singing "With a Little Help from My Friends" from Horrigan's own stereo.

"Good night, Frank. Stay in bed, now, till you shake those sniffles. . . ."

"Booth, wait—"

But the click told Horrigan his caller was gone; he returned the receiver to the hook, and waited. When the phone rang again, Agent Carducci was on the line.

"He scrambled it again," Carducci said. "We missed him."

Horrigan thought for a moment, mulling something Booth had said.

"I'm not so sure," he said.

"What do you mean?" Carducci asked.

"Nothing. Run me a cassette of that conversation. Have it over to my office by nine A.M."

"At the PPD?"

"No. I'll be back at Investigative Division, starting tomorrow."

He hung up, switched off the Beatles CD with the remote control, then, as an afterthought, got out of his chair and slipped a Miles Davis disc back in. He sat smiling as he listened to it.

Feeling much better.

The next morning, three blocks from the White House, at Secret Service headquarters, Horrigan sat at his desk in a cubicle office, listening to the cassette Carducci had sent over. Specifically, he was playing one excerpt for a young round-faced agent named Hopkins, who stood before his desk like the fresh-faced acolyte he was.

Booth's voice, slightly distorted, came from the small cassette player's speaker: "*Some people die because they do bad things. Some people die because they do good things. Others die simply because they're from Minneapolis.*"

The significance of this clearly eluded the young agent.

Horrigan said, "Contact the Minneapolis Field Office. Have them check into any murders or accidental deaths that might possibly tie into Booth. Particularly have them check around the time when the President took his campaign swing through Minneapolis/St. Paul. Fax them our entire Booth file, such as it is, to provide them context."

Hopkins nodded, and on the way out almost collided with Al D'Andrea, who came rushing in, excited.

"Wait till you hear this," D'Andrea began.

"First you listen to this," Horrigan said, and played him the tape excerpt. D'Andrea didn't seem any more comprehending than the junior G-man.

"Don't you get it?" Horrigan asked. "The son of a bitch is admitting a murder! It's a goddamn clue."

D'Andrea accepted this cheerfully. "If you say so. . . . You're making a believer out of me, I gotta admit. You just might be a genius."

"Yeah, but will I be recognized in my own lifetime? What have you got?"

D'Andrea pulled up a chair, grinned as he read from his spiral notebook. "You said check into model builders. Well, I found this professor at the University of Illinois, or I should say an Illinois Field Office agent, D'Orso, did. I read D'Orso's report, then spoke to the prof on the phone, myself."

"And?"

He tapped the notebook. "And this professor—Professor Riger—he teaches automotive design, works with students on various phases of designing and building model prototypes . . ."

"Like the ones in Booth's magazines."

"Right! In fact, there was an article about the professor and his futuristic prototypes in one of those magazines, which led Agent D'Orso to the prof, and—"

"Cut to the chase."

"Okay. The professor says he attended this design conference in New Orleans, about a year ago, and met this 'real oddball,' which I guess in these circles is saying something. According to the prof, both he and this guy got pretty well sloshed, and the oddball, who'd been pretty affable up to then, got real cranky when the subject of the federal government came up."

"Do tell."

"Prof says the guy got downright nasty. Said the government had 'betrayed' him . . ."

Booth's word.

" . . . *and* said he might just have to exact some measure of revenge."

Horrigan nodded slowly. "I don't suppose the professor remembers the oddball's name."

"Afraid not. But he did say he thought the guy hailed from San Antonio."

Perking, Horrigan sat up, said, "We're going to need a list of all the model and hobby shops in San Antonio. . . ."

D'Andrea's smile turned smug. "I've already called the Texas Field Office. It's being put together."

"*You're* the genius. How about contacting Agent D'Orso in Chicago, and getting a police artist sketch out of the professor?"

"That, too."

Horrigan stood behind his desk. "D'Orso can fax

it to us in San Antonio, 'cause that's where we'll be."

"That's what I told him." D'Andrea grinned, pleased with himself. "Our tickets are waiting at the airport."

19

Horrigan had D'Andrea drive the rental Ford Mustang. The younger agent had been here on a vacation, with his wife and son, less than a year before, San Antonio (or San Antone as the natives insisted on calling it) being a top tourist spot.

"Incredible zoo in this town," D'Andrea said, cheerful behind the wheel. "Sea World. The Alamo's here."

"I remember," Horrigan said, not giving a damn.

But he was relieved D'Andrea at least knew his way around a little, because the Texas town was confusingly laid out, streets crisscrossing the river and arranged in a circular fashion, not unlike Washington, D.C.

They'd made a connection at Dulles well before noon, and were driving around San Antonio by three-thirty. This would be a two-day job, though, because they surely wouldn't have time to check the half dozen hobby and model shops on their list before stores closed at five.

But they got lucky.

In the Riverwalk shopping area downtown, their first address turned out to be a trendy little cubbyhole in an old gutted-out building renovated for tourist shops; not surprisingly, they came up blank. Just before five, however, with the second name on their list—in a suburban strip mall—they hit the jackpot.

The shop was a dark, demented little place, messy enough to make Horrigan's apartment look like a *House Beautiful* magazine spread. Display models of cars, planes, rocket ships, movie monsters, hung twisting from ceiling wires, lurked on shelves among stacks of boxed kits, peeked from cluttered display cases. A corner workbench, under a harsh, gooseneck desk lamp, was scattered with various tools, machinery, glue tubes, sandpaper and just plain junk.

Walter Wickland, the proprietor, chewed gum as he leaned over one of the glass display counters, sneering at the fax Horrigan held out, of the Chicago police artist's sketch of Professor Riger's "oddball." He'd already given the man a look at the Colorado driver's license photo of "Joseph McCrawley."

Speaking of oddballs, pudgy, five o'clock–shadowed Wickland—wearing thick-lensed, heavy-framed glasses, a spattered canvas apron over a black T-shirt and jeans that didn't look worth protecting—seemed innately, pointlessly angry.

But what a sweetheart he turned out to be.

"Doesn't look exactly like him, and that photo looks like a relative or something—but it's *got* to be Mitch Fuckin' Leary."

Horrigan and D'Andrea exchanged glances. The younger agent jotted the name down in his spiral notebook.

"What can you tell us about him?" Horrigan asked.

"He's one crazy son of a bitch, that's what I can tell you about him. You looking for him?"

"Yes."

"Well, if you find the cocksucker, he's owed me money for over a year! Keep that in mind."

"Will do. What does he owe you for?"

Wickland shrugged, chewed his gum maniacally. "Tools. Couple kits. Car and a boat, I think. Motherfucker! Hope you throw him in the slammer till his dick rots off. Let me get you his address. . . ."

Smiling like an evil elf, Wickland hustled over to a file card box.

D'Andrea whispered: "Remind me not to owe this guy money."

Dusk was just threatening to fall as they drove along a pleasant, quiet residential street, windows down, enjoying the dry, cool breeze that riffled the leaves of the magnolias and mimosas lining the block. This mixture of frame and brick homes probably dated to the Fifties, yards tidy, well kept, the grass still green with just a tinge of yellowing. Here was a cactus garden. There a wagon-wheel flower garden. Next door, a front-yard patio with a hitching-post railing and a cutout barn-wood name plaque shaped like the head of a longhorn steer.

And then there was Mitch Leary's front yard.

Overgrown, unattended, tall grass battling with taller weeds, and losing. Next to the meticulous lawns on either side of the modest, off-white aluminum-sided home, the effect of this unruly mini-landscape was startling, even eerie.

Horrigan, with D'Andrea right behind him, walked up a cracked sidewalk that itself was being overtaken by wild grass; bits of branches and other debris littered it, as well. The curtains in the house were drawn. Nobody home, apparently.

But you never knew.

Horrigan's suit coat was unbuttoned, the revolver under his arm easily accessible, as he stood on the cement front stoop and tried the doorbell. No longhorn steer placard announced the Leary residence.

No answer.

Since he hadn't heard the bell ringing within, Horrigan tried knocking. Still no answer. He tried again, then gestured with a curled finger to D'Andrea—who seemed, frankly, a little rattled by this House of Weeds—to follow him around back.

Not surprisingly, the backyard was even more overgrown; a pecan tree had spilled its goodies, and a horde of squirrels were rustling and wrestling in the high grass, fighting over and feasting on the spoils. Horrigan got out his gun.

"Frank," D'Andrea whispered, clutching his partner's elbow, his worry palpable. "What's *that* for?"

"It's a key," Horrigan whispered back.

He chose a window and used the gun butt to shatter a pane; the glass, and gun butt, were cushioned slightly by the drawn curtain behind. He pushed his hand carefully through, working between the curtain and inner window to find the latch, which he did, then undid it and pushed the window up.

Because of the goddamn curtain, which he got half-tangled in, he didn't see the end table by the window as he crawled through, and he knocked it over, and tumbled to a carpeted floor, thank God not landing on any shards of window glass.

He couldn't believe how dark it was in the place— with every curtain drawn, it might as well have been midnight. Eyes barely adjusting, he was getting to his feet, taking in a routinely furnished, Holiday Inn– impersonal living room, dominated by a cobblestone fireplace, when he felt something cold and metallic in his ear.

The nose of a revolver.

The voice was quiet, soft, but menacing enough: "Stay right there. Don't even think about it."

A hand slipped inside Horrigan's coat and took his .38 away.

Horrigan risked a sideways glance, not moving his head, just his eyes. The guy was big, almost burly, but he had a baby face. Young, late twenties at the most. Business suit. Not a hood. Not Leary. Who the hell *was* this?

These thoughts took all of half a second; the next second-and-a-half belonged to D'Andrea, as he came through the same window, also getting half-tangled in the curtain and falling over the end table.

Inside, D'Andrea, on his hands and knees, looked up with wide eyes, frozen with fear and surprise.

All of this distracted the baby-faced gunman just long enough for Horrigan to whip his extendible baton from his belt and slash it toward his captor. The baton expanded to its full two feet, whapping the guy in the thigh, hard, giving him an instant charley horse, sending him to his knees with a yowl, gun popping out of his hand and bouncing beneath a chair several feet away.

Then Horrigan was behind the son of a bitch, using the baton to effect a choke hold; D'Andrea had finally got his gun out and was crouching, trembling, training it on his partner and his captor-turned-captive.

Horrigan kept the choke hold going just long enough to make the guy think he might die, then released the pressure and said, "And just who the fuck might you be?"

The guy was breathing hard—maybe he was stalling, maybe he was trying to talk, Horrigan wasn't sure. He hauled the guy to his feet and grabbed him by the suit coat, with two hands, and more or less repeated his question, nose to nose with the terrified gunman.

A voice behind them, not at all threatening, almost weary, said, "Let him go, Horrigan."

Horrigan whirled, pulling the gunless gunman around in front of him as a shield, yelling to D'Andrea, "Al?"

D'Andrea said, uncertainly, "I . . . I got him."

His partner was pointing his gun at a tall, cleancut, middle-aged man in a dark, well-tailored suit and a crisply knotted red tie with white stripes. He was as blandly, unmemorably handsome as a male model, but his eyes were a disturbingly dead cobalt blue.

Horrigan didn't know the guy, but he could smell what he was . . . and a sick feeling was crawling into his stomach. Not the flu, either, not this time.

"We're on the same side, Agent Horrigan," the man calmly said. Slowly, carefully, he raised his palm to reveal his I.D.

Horrigan walked his human shield over to have a look.

"Robert Coppinger," he said, livid, as he took in the CIA I.D. "Figured you for a Company man. What about Junior, here?"

"He's with me."

Horrigan let the baby-faced agent loose, shoving him roughly to one side. He approached Coppinger, stood just inches away; tightened his gaze and fixed it on him.

"Who are you here for, spook? Me or Leary?"

Coppinger's smile tried to be friendly but it was just patronizing. "Frank. Please. We're on the same team."

"You didn't answer my question."

The CIA man backed away with a grimace of a smile, took a seat—the easy chair the baby-faced gunman's revolver had spun under—and crossed his legs, casually.

"Mr. Leary," he said quietly, "used to belong to us."

That tore it. That fucking tore it. . . .

"Isn't that cozy," Horrigan said derisively. "Did you know your boy's threatened to kill the President?"

Coppinger frowned; he seemed almost embarrassed. His open handed gesture was awkward. "Yes, but . . . we didn't take him seriously. . . ."

"You *what*?"

"We didn't take him seriously—not until you turned up that fingerprint."

Horrigan's rage was bubbling, worse than his recent fever. "So that print *was* in the computer. Classified, was it? Fuck! Fuck you guys."

"Mr. Horrigan . . ."

"Isn't that sweet. You and the FBI—all you boys in bed together, in the great J. Edgar Hoover tradition."

Coppinger's frown got hostile, out around the edges. "We consider it an in-house problem."

"So screw the Secret Service? Well, this is an in-house problem, all right—but the house in question is *white*. Get me?"

Coppinger pursed his lips. "I get you. But we have certain . . . overriding concerns. If there were a public trial involving Leary, several key operations of ours would be compromised—"

"So you risk the President's life protecting them? Sure—makes sense to me. After all, what the hell—Presidents come and go, every four fuckin' years. If one dies, there'll be another one to take his place."

Coppinger sighed. Uncrossed his legs. "I understand your frustration."

"Frustration?" Horrigan raged. "My frustration? Why, you pompous sons of bitches . . . what did Leary *do* for you? Run coke to support the Contras? Sell arms to fucking Iran?"

Coppinger's face twitched. He glanced at the younger agent; then he cleared his throat and said, "This is off the record. Understood?"

Horrigan nodded. D'Andrea, whose glazed expression indicated just how in over his head he felt, did likewise.

"If asked we'll deny it," Coppinger said, arching an eyebrow.

Horrigan sneered. "Spill, already."

Another sigh. Long. Heavy. Coppinger said, "Leary is what these days we call a 'wet boy.'"

The words hit Horrigan like a physical blow. He swallowed thickly. Stumbled over to the couch and sat down.

D'Andrea was even more confused. "What? What are you guys talking about? What the hell's a 'wet boy'?"

Horrigan's voice sounded distant in his own ears. Distant and dead.

"Wet work, Al—blood," he said quietly. "Leary's a government-trained, professional assassin. . . ."

D'Andrea's eyes narrowed; his face whitened.

Coppinger rubbed the bridge of his nose, his eyes closed. "In Leary's case, that's putting it way too lightly. This man is. . . . He's more like a human predator."

The four agents—two Secret Service, two CIA—sat and stood in silence for what seemed like an eternity in the quiet little curtain-darkened suburban house. Outside, squirrels chattered, fighting for nuts.

Inside, a sense of dread settled on Frank Horrigan, who suddenly realized just who and what was he was up against.

20

●●●●●●●●●●●●●●●●●●●●●●●●●

The sun setting over the pond, streaming through these lush woods in western Maryland, turned the water's glassy surface a bright shimmering red, as if some terrible wound had been cut in the earth, and the spilled blood had gathered there.

At least that was how Leary, standing placidly on the shore wearing a pale green knit sweater and blue jeans, saw it; he held, in his left hand, a little remote-control pad, as he watched a sleek model boat he'd built in his basement workshop go skimming across the pond, its tiny motor making a cute, electric shaver–like sound.

Then he raised his right hand, aiming the squarish, cream-colored homemade pistol, its parts assembled, snapped snugly in place, but requiring this last simple, but crucial test. . . .

Birds were chirping, crickets called, and a shot cracked and shut them the fuck up, blowing the little remote-control boat to smithereens.

He liked that word. He said it aloud: "Smither-eens."

He inspected his gun, beaming at it with the approval a parent bestows on a gifted child; then, sticking the remote-control pad in a sweater pocket, he calmly watched the plastic pieces of his craft as they floated, scattered on the water's surface, and the birds began to chirp again, crickets began to call once more, and somebody's voice said, "Was that *you* shootin'?"

The two hunters, one in plaid, one in khaki, came rustling through the brush, rifles cradled in their arms.

One was heavyset and sort of fish-faced; the other was thin with birdlike features, particularly the sharp, prominent nose. Both were in their late twenties or possibly early thirties.

"That was me," Leary acknowledged with a gentle smile.

The hunter who'd spoken, the pudgy fish-faced one, grinned eagerly, curiously, as he noticed the cream-colored weapon in Leary's hand. "What the heck kinda gun is that?"

"Something I made at home."

"You *made* it?" the second hunter said, the bird-beaked one; his voice was as thin as he was.

"Sure."

Both hunters seemed impressed, glancing at each other and nodding their mutual endorsement of Leary's little science project.

"Can I see?" the second hunter asked.

"Why not?" Leary handed it to him.

The beaky guy took it, hefted it, poked his nose close, examining it as if relying on smell not sight;

· **170** ·

the motion reminded Leary of a chicken pecking.

"Awful lightweight," he said, doubtfully. "What's it made out of?"

"It's composite. A special type of resin I came up with."

The skinny hunter handed his pudgy companion the gun; he too hefted it, nodded. "Light as a feather. Sorta like plastic?"

"Yeah. Sorta like plastic."

"Pretty neat. Can I give 'er a try?"

Leary's gentle smile settled in one cheek. "Sure. There's a bullet left."

"Two shots, huh?"

"Mmm hmmm."

The skinny hunter looked around for a target. He spotted a bird on the opposite shore—about the size of a pigeon, dark with red markings, Leary didn't know what kind, he didn't know anything about birds—and fired.

The creature exploded in a burst of feathers and blood.

"Ha!" the skinny hunter said, and his pudgy friend was laughing, too. "Pretty *damn* neat! You wouldn't be interested in sellin' it, would you?"

"Why? It's not as good as your rifle."

"I'm kind of a collector. What say? Name your price—within reason, naturally."

Leary fished two bullets from his jeans pocket and broke the gun open carefully and reloaded. "No, I need it. It's for something special."

"Oh yeah?" the fish-faced one asked, grinning, full of curiosity. He should have looked like a cat, Leary thought. "Whatcha need it for?"

"To kill the President," Leary said, quietly matter-of-fact.

The two hunters laughed, but just briefly, as they suddenly seemed to be looking at Leary differently. The stillness of the forest—but for the birds chirping, and crickets calling—must have seemed very loud indeed to these two woodsmen.

"Why would you want to do that, mister?" the skinny one asked, his smile uneasy, hoping this was the sick joke it seemed to be.

Leary shrugged. "Why'd you kill that bird, asshole?"

He shot the pudgy one first.

Fanned out on the conference room table in Sam Campagna's office at the O.E.O.B. were five photos of Mitchell Andrew Leary.

Leary the high-school football player, trying to look mean.

Leary the grinning college frat-house member.

Leary the stone-faced young Army officer in fatigues in a Cambodian jungle.

Leary the beaming groom by his blushing beautiful brunette bride.

Leary the unshaven, slovenly subject of a surveillance photo.

The photos were spread out like a bizarre hand of cards; *all jokers*, Horrigan thought acidly. And what good did any of them do?

Sitting at the conference table with Horrigan and his partner D'Andrea were his boss Campagna himself, of course, CIA man Coppinger and one representative each from the FBI and the D.C. police. Horrigan knew both men slightly—Inspector Rawlins and Captain Howard.

"We've been trying to locate Leary for some time now," Coppinger said. "Maybe the FBI will have more luck than we have."

Rawlins, a dark-haired, rugged agent in his forties, said, "If we all work together, maybe so."

Horrigan looked up from the wedding photo he was studying to say, "Are you including the Secret Service in that? This time?"

Rawlins glared at Horrigan, then ignored the comment, saying, "With his fingerprints, and these photos, we—"

"What makes you think these photos are going to do us any good?" Horrigan threw the photo on the table and it slid into the others. "Most of these are at least fifteen years old. Newest one is almost ten years old, and blurry as hell. The Colorado driver's license I.D. is still our best bet."

Coppinger raised a skeptical eyebrow in agreement. "Men in Leary's line do tend to keep out of the camera's eye."

"No shit, Sherlock," Horrigan said. "Hell, he'll be in *disguise* anyway. . . . He's got spook training in that area, obviously—right? That's the downside of the Colorado pic."

Coppinger nodded.

"They're all worthless," Horrigan said, speaking directly to Campagna, pointing to the photos, "unless we get some first-rate computer alterations."

"I agree," Campagna said. He turned to the uniformed, white-haired, black-mustached Captain Howard. "Phil, I want you to tell your men Leary is a counterfeiter. We don't want the press getting hold of this."

Howard nodded. Then, examining the Army photo, he said bleakly, "I just can't understand why a man who served his country so honorably—a highly decorated soldier—would want to kill his own Commander in Chief. . . ."

"Honorably?" Horrigan asked. "How the hell much honor is there in 'wet work,' anyway?"

"Just what kind of man are we dealing with?" Campagna asked the CIA agent.

Coppinger's sigh spoke volumes. He bent to remove a manila folder from his briefcase. "Gentlemen, what I'm about to show you is highly classified. . . ."

He handed Horrigan two black-and-white photos.

"This man is a former colleague of Leary's—a close friend who, at our request, went to Leary's home in San Antonio to try to persuade him to accept counseling, and retraining."

The photos depicted a setting familiar to Horrigan—Leary's living room—but near the stone fireplace lay a man in suit and tie, his clothing, like his limbs, askew. The man's face was away from the camera, but Horrigan could get the picture, all right.

The guy's throat had been cut, ear to ear. Blood soaked the front of his shirt and the carpet nearby. The blood looked black in the picture, of course. But somehow that only made it seem redder.

"This, gentlemen," Coppinger said quietly, "is how Mitch Leary treats his *friends*. . . ."

By that evening, Horrigan was studying a baker's dozen of photo alteration printouts, provided by a very skillful female agent named Kopit back at the Intelligence Division computer center.

Using the color wedding photo, she had factored in eye color, facial hair, glasses, weight changes, skin coloration and, of course, the fifteen years since the photo was taken.

"Good as these are," Horrigan said, "they're no good at all."

D'Andrea, who'd been driving in silence, said nothing.

"There's no *life* to 'em. . . . Eyes are wrong. That's where you can spot a man best—his eyes. . . ."

D'Andrea nodded, barely.

Horrigan piled the photo printouts into their folder and said, "We need to find out more about these remote-controlled model kits and all. Now that we know Leary's had some ordnance background, that's crucial."

D'Andrea said nothing.

"First thing tomorrow," Horrigan began, "I want you to go to—"

"I'm resigning tomorrow."

Horrigan looked at D'Andrea, really looked at him, for the first time that evening; realized his partner hadn't just been quiet, but brooding.

"What's goin' on, pal?"

"I've just had it, that's all."

He searched D'Andrea's face. Thought for a moment. Then said, "Because you were scared in San Antonio?"

D'Andrea flinched, barely.

"Shit. I was scared, too. But you did your job. So did I."

"I was so fucking nervous . . ."

"Why shouldn't you be?"

"Frank, ever since . . . ever since they pulled that plastic bag over my head, I have nightmares."

Oh shit.

D'Andrea was watching the road but his eyes were seeing something else. "Every night, I'm back on that fucking boat. That guy's pulling that bag over my head, and I can't breathe, I'm dying, fucking dying. . . . Can you understand that, Frank?"

"Yeah."

"I feel like . . . it took the edge right off of me in San Antonio. You could have got killed, 'cause of me. I won't have that, Frank. I just won't fucking have it."

"We all have our nightmares, Al."

"I can't see you—"

"Dallas."

D'Andrea stopped short. His eyes closed for a moment. "Oh. I'm sorry. Should have—"

"There's counselors you can go to."

"Did you go to them?"

"Well, no . . ."

"It won't work for me, in any case." D'Andrea pulled over. "You want out here, or at the bar?"

"Here's fine." He touched his partner's arm. "Don't quit on me, Al. Stay with me on this. We're close to the bastard. We're so fucking close. We can get him. We *can* get him."

D'Andrea seemed to be weakening.

Horrigan pushed. "I need you, buddy! Let's not have any more of this cockamamie talk. . . ."

D'Andrea's brooding expression remained, but he said, softly, "Okay."

Horrigan opened the car door. Then he paused.

"There's a word for you—'cockamamie.' Your generation hasn't exactly embraced that one."

D'Andrea looked at him like he was insane.

"Liable to fade right out of the language. Be a damn shame, good word like that. Promise me something—use it now and then. Keep it alive, after your senile old partner is long gone."

D'Andrea was making a face. "Cockamamie?"

"Cockamamie."

D'Andrea blurted a laugh, shook his head, waved; Horrigan shut the door and watched his partner drive off.

"Made him laugh, anyway," he said to no one.

Then he changed his mind about going right home, and walked to the bar, where he sat and sipped Jameson and played "Just Friends," his back to the window.

Once, he had the strangest feeling someone was watching him, and turned, but no one was there.

If he had glanced around five seconds earlier, he'd have seen Mitch Leary.

21

In the Protective Division bullpen in the O.E.O.B., Horrigan was sitting at his desk going over Leary-related reports from various field agents when Lilly Raines appeared before him, like a vision. A vision in a pants suit with a mannish tie draped cutely around the open collar of her white mannish shirt.

"You weren't over at Investigative very long, were you?" she said, pleasantly.

It wasn't really a question, but he answered it anyway: "One day."

"That must be a record," she said, with a toss of her head. She was still wearing her hair down—he loved the way it swayed, brushing her shoulders.

"Yeah," he said, "then we turned up the Leary lead, and I've been back here ever since."

"Coming up with much?"

"According to our field agents, Leary's friends and his very frightened ex-wife say he's a nut."

She smirked wryly. "Film at eleven." Then the

smirk evolved into an awkward, almost shy smile. "Frank, I'm . . . glad you proved yourself right, on Booth. Leary."

"Thanks. Just striking a blow for senior citizens everywhere. How are you getting along without me? Still crying yourself to sleep every night?"

"Oh, it's been simply unbearable," she said facetiously.

"How long are you in town?"

"Just till tonight. I'm coordinating the advance for the California trip next week."

He whistled slowly. "Lead advance in L.A.? You *do* thrive on pressure."

"Like you don't?" She smiled—tenderly, he thought, or was that just wishful thinking?

About to go, she said, "Keep me posted on Leary. Sam has the number where you can reach me in L.A.—"

"It's the Bonaventure Hotel, right?"

"Right."

"Of course, we could have some coffee right now, and I could give you everything I've got, in detail. . . ."

She was thinking that over, apparently trying to decide if his double entendre was on purpose or not, when the phone rang and he gestured with a finger.

"Don't go," he said. "Just let me get this. . . ."

"Hello," the voice said.

His eyes told her it was Leary and she scurried to alert the other agents, but Carducci and Okura, their table of electronics gear back in operation, nodded at Horrigan, giving him twin high signs.

"Frank?" the familiar wispy voice asked innocently. "What are you doing? Giving everyone a chance to listen in?"

In fact, agents—including Sam Campagna himself—were gathered all around with headsets on. D'Andrea stood next to Lilly, listening intently.

"Would that surprise you?" Horrigan asked.

"Of course. Hello, everybody! But you know, it does rob us of . . . some of our intimacy."

Horrigan's sneer conveyed his nausea, and there were actually a few smiles in the audience of agents.

"By the way," Horrigan said offhandedly, "I know who you are, Mitch."

The silence that followed seemed endless.

Horrigan frowned. Was that a card he shouldn't have played? Would he now lose contact with his "friend," now that "Booth" was dead and Leary out of the closet?

Then the whispery voice was back: "Actually, it's about time you found out, Frank. I'm a little disappointed it took you *this* long. But in a way—I'm glad you know."

"Really? And why is that?"

"Isn't it obvious? Friends should be able to call each other by name. By their *real* names."

"Well, I have a little problem with that, Mitch."

"What, Frank?"

"We're not friends."

"Oh, of course we are."

"Well, let me put it this way: I don't want to be your friend, now that I know what you *do* to your friends."

The whispery quality in the voice evaporated; suddenly Leary's tone was razor sharp, and bitter as bile. "What did they *tell* you?"

"Just that you slit your friend's throat."

"That is *dis*-information, Frank! *Dis*-information! You should know better than to buy into that bull-shit. I'm *so* disappointed in you! God!"

"Photos don't lie, Mitch."

"Oh, sure they do—you saw only what those con-niving bastards *wanted* you to see—"

"I saw a man in your living room with his god-damn throat cut. Ear to fucking ear."

Leary's voice was trembling—part of it was fury, part of it something else.

"What you *didn't* see, Frank, what they *didn't* tell you, is that they sent my *best friend*, my brother in arms, a man whose fucking life *I* saved in fucking Cambodia *two* times . . . They sent *him* to kill *me*."

"Why is your voice shaking, Mitch? You aren't crying, are you?"

"Now you're trying to hurt me. What have I ever done to you? I've never lied to you, not once. And you know what? I never will."

"Tell me one thing, Mitch—why is it that every-one who ever knew you says you're one sick son of a bitch? Your friends, your colleagues, your wife . . ."

"What does *your* wife have to say about *you*, Frank?"

"We're not talking about me, Mitch."

Leary really did sound like he was weeping, now. "You . . . You of all people, Frank. I thought you would understand. I still *want* you to under-stand. . . ."

"Why should I make any effort to understand some poor sick son of a bitch?"

A long pause. Horrigan glanced over at Carducci, hunkered in his headset over the electronics gear, his eyes saying: *Not yet. Not yet. . . .*

Leary's voice returned and it was the gentle whisper again: "You should understand me, Frank, because we both used to think this country was something pretty damn special."

"You don't know what I used to think. Mitch, you don't know a damn thing about me. . . ."

"And what do you know about me, what do you *think* you know about me, now that the files with their lies have been opened to you? You know what I did for them? What I *really* did for them? In the service of my country? I let them take me like clay and mold me any way they wanted. They transformed me into something . . . terrible. Hell, I don't remember, now, who I even was before they got their claws into me. Frank, I did some horrible things, for God and country . . . and I was given medals and I was given commendations and they even paid me handsomely. More than you Secret Service bums, I'll bet. But you know what, Frank?"

"What, Mitch?"

"The day came when they had no use for the monster they made. So they decided to destroy it. 'Cause we can't have monsters roaming the great American countryside, now can we?"

"Tell me something, Mitch."

"What, Frank?"

"What do you see when you dream?"

This time it was Horrigan who had pushed a button.

Leary exploded: "I see *you*, Frank. I see you standing over the grave of *another* dead president!"

Horrigan reeled for a second—Leary still knew

how to push a button or two, himself. He glanced at Lilly, listening on her headset, and she gave him a tight, encouraging smile. D'Andrea's expression was warm, supportive.

"That's not gonna happen," Horrigan said, with utter certainty. "I'm onto you, Mitch. You and your kid games."

"*Fuck* you, Frank! *Fuck* you! There's no way you or any fucking body can stop me. Not when I'm willing to trade my life for his! And I'm going to fuck your life up in the bargain. You know *why*? Why does a hunter shoot a bird? You know *how*? 'Cause I got the smarts and I got the guts and that's all it fucking takes, pal!"

"Give it up, Mitch. Give yourself up."

One harsh laugh. "So I can live a long and fruitful life in the land of the free?"

"You were a government agent. You have certain rights. I can see to it that you get help."

"A little help from my friends, Frank?"

"I guarantee it. Give me a chance. We'll work something out."

Horrigan's attempt to soothe Leary brought forth another explosion, more violent than the first: "Don't you fucking *lie* to *me*! I'm a dead man, and you know it! I was dead the day they sent my best friend to kill me. I'm the deadest man you know, except for the President. And *you*, Frank. If you get too close to me—"

Carducci was sitting up, smiling; he made a thumbs-up gesture.

Horrigan said, "You're losing it, Mitch."

The quavering voice seemed to vibrate between gentle and savage: "Do you have even the faintest notion, Frank, of how easily I could kill you? You can't imagine how many times I've watched you go in and out of your apartment. How about the night you and your girlfriend sat on the steps at the Lincoln Memorial licking ice-cream cones?"

Lilly almost gasped.

Leary ranted on: "You are alive, Frank, only because *I* allow *you* to live. So *show* me some goddamn *respect*!"

The click of Leary hanging up was simultaneous with Horrigan swiveling in his chair, to see Carducci shouting, "St. Francis Hotel! Florida Avenue—" as the bullpen came alive.

This time D'Andrea was the first one out the door, with Horrigan on his heels.

22

●●●●●●●●●●●●●●●●●●●●●●●●

D'Andrea hit the horn, blaring a path for his speeding Sunbird through an intersection and its red light, while Horrigan, riding with no seat belt, hung on with one hand to the top of the car through his open window, teeth gritted, tie fluttering in the wind.

"Slow down a little," Horrigan said, pointing. "There it is. . . ."

Up ahead, a trio of D.C. police squad cars were scattered at odd angles in the street, as if abandoned there, as scurrying uniformed cops and plainclothes officers converged on the rundown brick building, its rusted, battered, sideways ST. FRANCIS HOTEL neon advertising a long-gone era, when it was something more than a fleabag flophouse.

But as D'Andrea slowed and Horrigan looked up ahead, the younger agent noticed something out his side window and called, "Frank!"

On the other side of the street, a guy of medium height and build was walking briskly down the sidewalk, in the opposite direction from the hotel:

unshaven, he was hunched over, his clothes baggy and threadbare—black golf cap, brown work coat, loose gray jeans that flapped, as he walked, with the wind.

He looked like just another transient, in this rundown neighborhood, or possibly even some homeless street person.

Except for one thing.

"That bum's wearing sunglasses, Frank!"

"Yeah," Horrigan said. "Let's do it. . . ."

D'Andrea spun the wheel and the car around, and the guy—Leary, no question about it!—heard them, saw them, and began to sprint. D'Andrea was coming right up on him, Leary throwing a wild-eyed glance over his shoulder before cutting down an alley in mid-block.

The Sunbird squealed around, careened into the alley after him, but a junker car was blocking the way.

"Watch it!" Horrigan called, but the brakes were already squealing. They stopped an inch or two from the junker, and piled out, revolvers in hand.

"Nice work, partner," Horrigan said.

"Thanks," he said, but D'Andrea was frustrated, literally going around in circles, looking around the narrow alleyway for Leary and seeing nothing but garbage cans and debris and a cat eating a fish head. Front and back of the junker car were empty, Horrigan noted.

"Where the hell did he go, Frank?"

Horrigan heard metal whining above him, looked up, and pointed. "There!"

Leary was right above them, scrambling up an ancient fire escape.

Horrigan tried to jump up to grab and pull down the counterbalanced fire-escape stairs, but he couldn't make the reach.

"Give me a boost!" he ordered D'Andrea, and D'Andrea cupped his hands and Horrigan stepped up and flung himself onto the wrought-iron landing. He scrambled to his feet and flew up the rickety steps, two at a time, heart pounding, chest heaving, the dark shape of Leary above him like a wraith he was pursuing. Somehow he clattered his way up the five stories till he was up on the cracked black tar of the roof, getting there just in time to see that fucking Leary, on the run, leap to the roof of the adjacent building, land nimbly and dash on, blocked now from Horrigan's view by a battered ventilation duct.

With no thought whatsoever, Horrigan went after him—in a jog that grew into a hard run, legs churning, and as the edge of the building approached, he leapt!

Landed in a pile, rolled, got to his feet, gun still clenched firmly in his fist, and kept up pursuit, seeing Leary up ahead, the son of a bitch scared now, eyes darting back furtively as he streaked across the tar roof, dodging the obstacle course of exhaust vents and wire-mesh drains, nearing the edge of this building, and now Horrigan smiled.

The building next door wasn't close enough to jump to. He *had* the son of a bitch, now! Horrigan slowed just a little, relaxing his heavy breathing—

And the son of a bitch jumped, and—*fuck!*—made it to the other side!

Goddamn it! Horrigan thought, and shoved his revolver in his shoulder holster, and picked speed back up, legs pumping, veins throbbing in his forehead, flinging himself full-throttle, flying across the alley, diving toward that roof.

Landing short.

He'd have yelled *shit!* if he'd had the time or presence of mind to. It was all he could do to make his hands reach for the edge of that decaying rooftop, and clamber for dear life as his body slammed forcefully, painfully, into the side of the brick building, knocking what little wind he had left right the fuck out of him, his brain going black for an instant, but he made himself hold onto consciousness, just as his hands held onto the precarious, crumbling brick lip of the rooftop.

Muscles in his arms pulling and stretching like taffy, he dangled there, wind riffling his thinning hair. *Is this how I die?* he thought. *Crushed on the floor of some shit-infested slum alley?* He gulped a breath and risked a look down: the five-story drop seemed endless. *Where was D'Andrea? Did he chickenshit out?*

Over to the right, two stories down, was a fire-escape landing. He could survive *that* fall—that fall would be as easy as letting go . . . but he was a good three feet shy of it. And he couldn't hazard swinging over, not with the unstable grip he had on bricks that wiggled under his hands like loose baby teeth.

Maybe, though, they were secure enough for him to pull himself up. His feet kicked at the wall, like a hanged man's reflexive farewell, as his arms vainly tried to haul his leaden body up, but the muscles in his arms were weak, too busy burning to respond.

It was all he could do to hang on. He wanted to cry. He laughed.

"What's so funny, Frank?"

Looking down with bland condescension, the sunglasses off but the black cap still on, a blue-black revolver in one hand, was an unshaven, rather puffy-looking Mitch Leary.

Horrigan could barely speak; too short of breath. Too afraid.

But he managed, "If . . . if you're going to step on my . . . my fingers, Mitch . . . why don't you do it . . . get it . . . the hell over with."

Leary hunkered down, like a grown-up kneeling to speak to a child; the wind up here made his worn, baggy apparel flap like flags. He shook his head slowly and made the *tch tch* sound.

"How could you even think such a thing, Frank?" Leary reached out.

"Take my hand, Frank. Go on. Take it."

Horrigan looked up at the open-palmed offering as if it were some strange abstract object. From this perspective, the hand seemed huge. Like a grotesque movie prop.

Leary's smile was tiny and teasing, and he said, singsongily, "If you don't . . . you'll die."

The mortar holding the wobbly bricks under Horrigan's grip began to crumble, to completely give way, and with a gasp, Horrigan reached out desperately for Leary's hand, found it, grasped it, and now Leary's left hand was gripping him as he dangled, the only thing keeping Horrigan from dropping to that alley floor.

Above him, Leary smiled down benignly, like a priest about to bestow a blessing—a closemouthed smile, no teeth, just dimples and bright, dead eyes.

Even with the wind whipping him, even with his every muscle stretched to the breaking point, even with the hard drop of death waiting below his swaying feet, Horrigan was struck by the thought of this first physical link to a madman he'd known only on the phone, a madman he'd sworn to stop, but who had *him*, now.

Or did he?

Breathing slightly more easily, his right hand tight in Leary's grasp, suspended five deadly stories above the ground, Horrigan reached his left hand around and withdrew the .38 from the shoulder holster and pointed it up at the crazy bastard who was giving him a helping hand.

Leary seemed more hurt than surprised, but then a one-sided smile, as if he were tickled by the turn of events, settled in Leary's left cheek. "You're going to *shoot* me, Frank? After I saved your life?"

Straining, Horrigan gripped the gun tight; he wasn't as good with his left hand as his right, but he was good enough. Good enough to rid the world of this bastard, and protect the President one last time. . . .

Leary read his thoughts, saying, "That *is* the only way, Frank—the only way for you to save the President. Shoot me. Shoot me *now*."

Sweat ran into Horrigan's eyes and he didn't have a hand to brush the salty droplets away; he blinked, trying to make the blurry image of Leary leaning down over him stay in focus.

The taunting words floated down like acid-rain snowflakes: "Are you willing to do that? To trade your life for his? Or is it still too precious to you, your little life?"

His hand, his left hand, was shaking as he pointed the gun up at his demented savior; *fuck it,* Horrigan thought, and his finger was squeezing on the trigger when Leary frowned, reading his mind again, perhaps, and swung Horrigan out and away from the wall, and he was falling!

The feeling was oddly exhilarating, he felt free, and scared shitless. . . .

He landed with a hard, clanging thud on the crosshatch metalwork of the fire escape, twelve feet below. Leary's action, swinging him out like that, had saved him, inadvertently, possibly—but saved him.

But on the ride down, he had lost his gun—it was careening through space, and he heard its *klunk!* on the bricks three stories below.

Leary smiled down, eyes orgasmic. "We'll never know, now, will we, Frank? If you *really* had what it takes?"

"*Leary!*"

D'Andrea's voice!

Horrigan looked up and over, and there, on the adjacent rooftop, stepping out from behind an oversize ventilation duct, was D'Andrea, gun in hand, pointing it across at Leary. Al must have positioned himself there, and witnessed the entire confrontation, but what could he have done? Had he shot Leary, Horrigan would have dropped to his death.

Horrigan, breathing with relief, and pain from his drop, was proud of his partner; the young agent had played it right. Every step of the way today, right down the line, D'Andrea had been a real pro.

"Don't fucking *move*, Leary!" D'Andrea was saying.

Horrigan hauled himself up, leaning against the rail, where he could see Leary, whose hands were up. Where was that gun? Still in his hand?

"You okay, Frank?" D'Andrea said, glancing down at his partner; his pride, in coming through like the cavalry, in beating the fear bug, was evident in D'Andrea's tight little smile, but in that same split second, Horrigan wanted to call and warn him—

Too late.

The little gun was still in Leary's hand, and a killing machine like that only needed the fraction of an instant D'Andrea's proud glance had provided.

"Al!" Horrigan cried out. *"Al!"*

Much too late. Split second too late. Lifetime too late.

Three shots, rapid-fire, and Special Agent Albert Riccardo D'Andrea's head exploded in a Dallas-like blossom of blood and brain and bone, and his lifeless body tumbled back on the rooftop, out of Horrigan's sight.

Leary was gone, too.

Horrigan was alone.

Alone on the fire escape with the wind and his aches and pains and the sound of a scream echoing down the alley.

His.

23

•••••••••••••••••••••••••••••

The bartender at Horrigan's neighborhood watering hole was named Joe. Even Joe—round-faced and balding, with a wispy Zapata mustache and a cheerful but low-key demeanor—knew what a cliché that was. But it couldn't be helped. His name was Joe, he was a bartender, and that was all there was to it.

Some things, you just couldn't do anything about.

Horrigan sat slumped at the bar with a glass of Jameson—an inch of the stuff, which had started out as two inches—and the bottle in front of him.

Rather have a bottle in front of me, he thought, *than a frontal lobotomy.* Such an old joke. Always made him smile, though.

Not tonight.

Joe polished a glass and said, "You haven't played any piano tonight."

"No."

"Not in the mood?"

"No."

"You've been sitting here an hour, Frank, with that bottle in front of you."

"I'd rather have a bottle in front of me," Horrigan mumbled.

"You haven't poured yourself any—just that first glass."

"I know."

Joe started polishing another glass. "How come?"

"These days, I only drink in moderation."

"Then why do you want the bottle in front of you?"

"In case I change my mind." He pushed the bottle toward the bartender. "Pour yourself one."

"Okay." Joe shrugged, and did.

Horrigan raised his inch of whiskey. "Join me in a toast?"

"Sure. Who to?"

"A kid named Al I used to know."

He would talk to Al's wife, later. Pay his respects. What was her name? Something poetic, wasn't it?

Ariana.

He covered his face with a hand and wept into it. Joe went back to washing glasses and gave him some privacy. On the TV above the bar, the local news was covering the story, not giving it much attention. Death of a Secret Service agent was news in this town, but when a "counterfeiter" was responsible, it didn't stay news for long.

Which was how the Protective Division wanted it. Letting the press get wind of Leary would be a disaster.

He pounded a fist on the counter. *Why the fuck had he talked D'Andrea out of resigning?* Al would be alive now, if it wasn't for him; home with his

· **196** ·

son Ricky and his wife Ariana, home and alive and well and happy.

Maybe *he* should resign.

Maybe he would.

After he caught this evil cocksucker.

In Leary's hotel room, Brady, the fingerprint technician whose Omniprint 1000 had turned up Leary's palm print on that car they'd impounded, found a notepad by the phone, with some hand-scrawled, cursive letters. "SW SKELLUM LA."

Jack Okura had handed Horrigan a photostat. "It's Leary's handwriting, all right—CIA confirmed it. But neither they nor us or anybody can figure out what the hell it means."

Horrigan frowned at the note. " 'LA' could be Los Angeles, obviously—the President's next campaign stop. But what's 'skellum'? Foreign word?"

Okura nodded. "An old Dutch word—still in use in South Africa. Means a rascal, or a rogue. Specifically, it means: 'one deserving to die.' "

"Maybe it's how Leary signs his name," Horrigan said dryly.

Hours later, in the bar, Horrigan took the photostat from his pocket, unfolded it and again studied the jagged handwriting of the man who had killed his partner. He tried to make the phrase make some sort of sense, keeping in mind Leary's ironic bent; but nothing came.

He didn't hear the phone ring, and when Joe came over, to say, "Frank? You got a call," it surprised him.

He moved down a few stools, to where Joe had pulled the phone up onto the counter, and said hello.

"I'm sorry, Frank," the wispy, whispering voice said.

Something like sorrow seemed to tinge the words; or something like someone who once knew what sorrow was, and was trying to remember it, and emulate it.

"It was self-defense, Frank. I'm really so sorry."

Horrigan felt the blood drain from his face; his muscles tensed, his jaw tightened, veins bulged in his forehead, and Joe—washing glasses—looked up at him, and did a *Jesus!* of a double-take.

"It was him or me," Leary explained, reasonably.

Shaking, white-hot with rage, Horrigan made his voice sound calm. "Tell me about 'skellum.'"

Sharing the clue with the madman was a calculated risk, but Horrigan was in a risk-taking mode; he waited through a long pause, eager to gauge Leary's answer.

"Skellum's worthless. You're barkin' up the wrong tree, Frank. It's way late in the game, my friend, and you're just too far behind on points."

"No, Mitch. I'm ahead."

"How do you figure?"

"I know what you look like. I've seen the dead man in your eyes."

"How poetic, Frank!"

"Like the name Ariana."

"What?"

"That's the name of my late partner's wife. The man you murdered yesterday?"

"Maybe . . . maybe my eyes will look different next time."

"Contact lenses won't help. Your sick evil twisted fucking brain will still shine right through."

Another pause.

"You *are* angry with me," Leary said.

"I know who you are, I know what you are, and I know I'll find you. And when I do—"

"You'll kill me, Frank?"

"Bingo."

Leary chuckled. "Can't you feel it, Frank? The irony's so thick, you could choke on it."

"There's nothing ironic about me putting a bullet in your brain, Mitch. Poetic, maybe."

"No, it's *irony*, Frank—*think!* The same government that trained me to kill, trained you to protect. Yet I protected you, on that rooftop, while now *you* want to kill *me*! That's Irony 101, page one of the textbook, pal!"

"Shut up, Mitch."

"They're going to write books about us, Frank."

"Maybe, but I'm not going to read 'em."

"Why not, Frank?"

"Because I'm sick of you and all your bullshit, Mitch."

The *tch tch* sound. "You're such a poor sport. You had your chance, you know—your moment of truth. You could've taken me out, if you'd been quick enough—just like Dallas. But you hesitated—'cause your precious ass was on the line. Well, you made your choice, Frank. Quit cryin' in your beer!"

Horrigan slammed the phone down.

Joe lifted an eyebrow. "You okay?"

"No. If that asshole calls back, tell him you're tracing him and he'll leave you alone."

Joe swallowed. "Sure, Frank."

Horrigan finished his Jameson, threw a five spot

· **199** ·

on the counter, told Joe good night and headed out onto the street.

The air was nippy; his breath smoked. He needed more than just the suit coat he was wearing. He crossed his arms, huddling into himself as he walked toward his apartment. Up ahead, a man—his back to Horrigan—was using the phone in the booth.

Booth?

Leary?

Horrigan picked up his step, reached a hand under his arm and was about to pull out his revolver when the man turned and he was young, mustached, possibly gay, absolutely not Leary.

With a sigh, not returning the man's wink, Horrigan walked on, rage festering. In his apartment, he punched up the Beatles CD again, sat in his chair studying a copy of the lyrics to track 2, which he'd copied off the record, listening, trying to make sense of them. Find in them Leary's fucking irony.

Couldn't.

He wadded them up and pitched the crumpled ball of them across the room. Aimed the remote, angrily, at the CD player and shut off the song, like he was firing a gun.

The phone rang and he said, "Fuck you, Leary!"

Only it was Okura.

Embarrassed, Horrigan made a few notes as he learned from the agent that no one, in the entire greater Los Angeles area, was named Skellum.

"Well, how about Louisiana? Try there."

"We thought of that. Zip."

"Shit."

"We'll keep trying things."

"Good. Good night, Okura."

"You okay, Frank? This is awful rough, losing Al . . ."

"Not as rough as on the family."

He hung up.

He sat in the dark apartment, not listening to music, for a long, long time, finally falling asleep in his chair.

This time the dream was not the same.

Hot beautiful day in Dallas, gliding along on the running board of the follow-up car, everything in newsreel black and white, the sound of a firecracker, only it wasn't a firecracker, and he saw the figure slumped in the car, up ahead, and froze as the second shot hit the man in the limo, his head exploding in a bloody burst.

But this time the man in the limo wasn't Jack Kennedy.

It was D'Andrea.

24

At the head of the conference table in his office in the West Wing of the White House, Harry Sargent was standing, waving his arms like a demented member of a ground crew guiding in aircraft. Trying to stay calm in the center of the chief of staff's storm were the others seated at the table: Sam Campagna, Bill Watts, Lilly Raines and an unlikely guest in Sargent's office—Frank Horrigan.

"The election is in three weeks," Sargent was saying, eyes round and incredulous, "and you're asking me to keep the President *out* of Cali-fucking-fornia?"

"That's what we're asking, yes," Campagna said calmly, arms folded across his bearlike chest.

Sargent had a bearlike frame, too, and with his waving arms, he might have been about to pounce, grizzly-like. "Don't you realize . . . You're asking me—you're asking your President—to commit political suicide!"

"It's better than the other kind," Horrigan said softly.

Sargent's nostrils flared; he obviously resented Horrigan's presence. Ignoring the agent, he turned back to Campagna. "Do I have to tell you that California is the key to the whole damn race? Every mother's son knows that!"

"Including Leary," Horrigan said.

"That's the point," Lilly added.

Horrigan gave her a little sideways smile; having her support on this felt good.

Sargent was shaking his head; his face looked pouchy, the slicked-back Nixon hair staying in place, but his jowls were quivering in a Nixon-like manner, too.

"We've closed the gap in California to five points," he said. "We *can't* let up now. . . . We have no choice: we *gotta* go there. Those are the electoral votes that can cinch the thing."

He sat, heavily, as if that closed the subject.

Horrigan leaned forward, said, with a tentative gesture, "Then we have to radically change procedures."

Sargent glowered at the agent. "Such as?"

Horrigan shrugged. "Move him in unmarked cars, no motorcade, no pomp. Frisk anybody who could get closer than fifty yards to—"

Sargent's eyebrows shot up. "Frisk supporters at ten-thousand-dollar-a-plate dinners? There you go again."

The paraphrase of the Reagan line wasn't lost on Horrigan.

Softly, menacingly, the agent said, "What does that mean?"

"It means," the chief of staff said through his teeth, "that once again, Horrigan, *typically*, you're overreacting."

"If I *don't* overreact, the President's dead. Leary's a government insider, for Christ's sake. He knows our normal procedures. That, by definition, makes them ineffective, inoperative—"

Sargent wasn't really listening; he was shaking his head again, his darkly bagged eyes filled with contempt. "Maybe if we weren't still trying to gloss over the embarrassment you caused in Chicago . . ."

"We *could* make some procedural changes," Watts offered.

Sargent glared at the President's favorite bodyguard. "Don't tell me *you're* siding with this crank!" He waggled his finger at Watts accusingly. "I told you to keep this crazy man away from me—"

Campagna interjected, forcefully: "Frank Horrigan is heading up this investigation. He's been right about Leary from Day One. I would suggest you listen to him."

Taken aback by the rebuke, the chief of staff looked at the assistant director in charge of Presidential Protection, as if trying to decide whether or not to pull rank and lash back.

Instead, Sargent seemed to collapse, a little— shoulders hunched, he folded his hands; he might have been praying, but his bleak expression was strictly atheist.

"Look, people . . . " he said somberly; suddenly almost humble. "I sometimes forget we're all on the same team. I'm gonna level with you. I want you to understand what I'm up against: this *isn't* my call."

Horrigan glanced at Lilly and her expression was as grave as he imagined his was. Campagna looked ashen, and Watts's gaze was lowered.

"The *President* has already made this decision," Sargent said glumly. "He says he would rather die than lose."

Silence draped the room like a widow's black shawl.

Then, in quiet, reasoned words and tone, the chief of staff discussed with the Secret Service the extent to which standard operating procedures could be modified and improved upon for this vital—and dangerous—trip.

That night, at his desk in the O.E.O.B., Horrigan sat studying the "SW SKELLUM LA" photostat; on his notepad, he tried a reverse spelling, played anagram games with it—nothing. His desk was littered with new computer-generated photo alterations of Leary.

At the sound of footsteps in the nearly empty office, he glanced up and saw Lilly approaching him; he loved her fluid walk, the way she could make a mannish pants suit flow like an evening gown.

He smiled gently. "Agent Raines."

"Agent Horrigan," she said, smiling back the same way. She leaned a hand on his desk. "I got a message you wanted to see me."

"Sit down, would you?" He pulled a chair over for her, around alongside his desk, and she sat, crossing her legs, waiting patiently.

He continued, trying not to sound desperate as he said, "I want to assist you on the L.A. advance."

She didn't quite frown, but her reluctance was apparent.

"Why the long face, Lil? You were on my side in Sargent's office, today."

She chose her words carefully. "I think . . . maybe you're too close to this."

"Too close to *you*, you mean."

"Actually, that's not what I mean. Too close to Leary."

He edged his chair nearer to her. "That's just why I want to be there, Lil. I can spot him, anticipate him. Nobody else can, really."

"Frank . . ." This was clearly hard for her. "Even Bill Watts has come around to your way of thinking, at least to some degree. But what Sargent said about you overreacting . . . it's a concern shared by more than just Sargent."

"Is it shared by you, Lil?"

She answered indirectly: "I'm worried about the President."

"You should be. I am."

"That's not what I mean. This L.A. trip is crucial to his reelection. And you . . . you said yourself, you don't give a damn if he's humiliated or not."

He shrugged. "I say a lot of things when I lose my cool."

"Lately you lose your cool a lot, Frank."

He sighed; tried not to show either his frustration or his growing irritation. "Lil, if this is about you thinking I want to go to L.A. to get close to *you*—"

"I never said that."

"No, but isn't that what you're really afraid of? Me making another pass? Or is it that you might want to catch it?"

Her face flushed. "Sometimes you're so goddamn arrogant . . ."

"Like you're so brutally honest. Well, I admire that. So tell me—in all brutal honesty—that you not wanting me along has nothing to do with *us*—and I'll believe you. I'll take a pass. The other kind."

Her shoulders slumped and a tired smile tickled her lips. "All right . . . maybe it does have a little to do with 'us.' After all, I'm lead advance for a major Presidential campaign swing. You know what an overwhelming job that is."

"And you can't afford any distractions."

"Right."

"Well, what if I promise not to be one? I want to work with you on this, Lil. Strictly professional. Please."

"I don't know . . ."

He wanted this; he needed this. For himself. For D'Andrea.

He leaned forward and touched her hand. "Please," he repeated. "Besides, how can you miss this chance? Working with a living legend? The only active agent who ever lost a President."

She winced at that. Then she drew in a long breath, and let it out the same way. Moved her hand around from under his until she was holding it, squeezed it, let go, stood, walked away.

Look back, Lil, he thought. *Look back . . .*

She did, to smile and grant him a reluctant nod. But a nod.

"Thank you, Lil," he said, when she was gone.

That night, at Dulles airport, a prosperous-looking traveller, who any reasonable person would have taken for a top executive, was on his way to catch a red-eye to Los Angeles.

The man wore dark-rimmed glasses, was black-mustached, deeply tanned, slightly potbellied; his suit was tailored, clearly expensive, his briefcase leather. He wore a black toupee so expertly suited to the shape of his skull that the president of the Hair Club for Men wouldn't have recognized it for the camouflage it was.

Perhaps the only thing off-kilter about this apparently prominent businessman was revealed when he went through airport security's metal detector, setting it off.

Emptying his pockets of change and such into the tray provided him, the man traveling as James Carney deposited also a lucky rabbit's-foot key chain, a kitschy item which perhaps might have seemed incongruous for so distinguished-looking a traveler, had any of the security people given it a thought.

Which they didn't.

25

The Bonaventure Hotel was a nice place to visit, Horrigan thought, but he wouldn't want to protect the President there.

That, of course, was exactly what he was in the process of preparing to do. Right now, he was prowling the huge lobby with its myriad of glass-enclosed elevators, wishing the President had chosen any hotel but this one for his fund-raising dinner. The convention hotel, on South Figaro in downtown L.A., was at once vast and, with its maze of nooks and crannies, claustrophobic. Glancing up, he could see, from any angle, half a dozen places a sniper could perch.

They'd arrived yesterday morning, a PI (protective intelligence) team consisting of himself and Lilly, joined by a handsome young agent from the L.A. Field Office, Miguel Chavez. Utilizing local agents, he and Lilly had overseen bomb sweeps of bridges on the motorcade route; seen to it that mailboxes on the President's route were removed; that manhole covers were taped securely shut. They had driven through the route with members of the LAPD brass, with many stops along the way to discuss counter-sniper roof positions.

Last night, to an audience of LAPD officers assigned to hotel duty, he'd shown slides of both the full spectrum of computer-generated alteration images of Leary, and the lookouts known to be in the Los Angeles area. The latter comprised a Watch List of thirty-six names and faces.

This morning, Lilly and Chavez had gone to the Air Force landing base where two large military cargo planes set down, bringing in, literally, tons of communications and surveillance gear, which were loaded into unmarked vans. Also rolling out of the cargo planes were four limousines, one of them the President's own.

At the same time, Horrigan had been supervising the technical agents who were sweeping the Presidential suite for bombs and bugs. A German shepherd sniffed suspiciously, while humans removed vents, lifted up rugs and X rayed the walls.

Things were going smoothly, but Horrigan was on edge. The hotel seemed a poor choice, logistically; an ideal place for Leary to make his move. Restless, he tried to get a better sense of the massive lobby. He stayed away from a TV newswoman in the process of taping a report; wandered toward the other side of the lobby, where Lilly, clipboard in hand, was taking a roll call of the several dozen field agents, men and women of every ethnic variety, who were playing roles in this little Presidential melodrama—some "guests," others hotel "employees."

Just to his left, a hotel bellboy was waiting for an

elevator. He had no bags in hand. Where was he going? What was he up to? Horrigan moved toward him. The guy was about twenty-five, dark-haired, pockmarked.

The bellboy glanced over at Horrigan, noticed him looking, and began to fidget, tapping his foot nervously, waiting for the elevator.

Horrigan's eyes narrowed as he fumbled through his suit-coat pocket and came up with the stack of Watch List photos; he thumbed through, quickly found the one he wanted: Paul Rubiak. Mental patient—whereabouts unknown—threatening letters to the President. Dark-haired. Pockmarked. Twenty-six.

The bellboy.

Horrigan spoke into his cuff-mike: "Lilly, I got a Watch Lister at elevator nine. Paul Rubiak . . ."

The elevator doors were sliding open. The bellboy was about to step on.

"Hold it up, there!"

Horrigan moved in quickly, yanking his gun from under his arm, flashing his badge.

"What . . . ?" The bellboy backpedaled, looking panicky.

"Freeze," Horrigan snapped. "Secret Service!"

Slipping his badge back in his pocket, Horrigan grabbed the bellboy's arm, but the guy pulled away, angrily, saying, "Hey! I *work* here, pal!"

Horrigan gave him a gentle jab in the balls, and as the bellboy grimaced in pain, Horrigan spun him around, and shoved him against the wall.

Gun back in his shoulder holster, Horrigan was frisking the guy when Lilly and several other agents rushed up.

"Frank . . . ?" Lilly began.

Horrigan had the bellboy's wallet out and was looking at a California driver's license with photo I.D. and the name Robert Stermer.

Lilly was quickly checking a computer printout on her clipboard. "Robert Stermer. He's a bellboy. He's been cleared."

Robert Stermer, bellboy, turned around; he was still wincing from the jab in the nuts.

"What's wrong with you, man?" he managed.

"Sorry," Horrigan said, with a tight smile. "Have a nice day."

Lilly touched his arm. "Don't look now, but we have company. . . ."

He glanced around to see the newswoman with microphone in hand, backed up by a cameraman with his portable on his shoulder. They were both grinning. Happy to have caught what they just caught. . . .

"Can you explain what just happened here?" the newswoman began.

Agent Chavez, who was handling press relations, intervened—thank God—politely steering the team to one side, as Horrigan and Lilly made their getaway.

"*You* saw the Watch List picture," Horrigan said.

"Strong resemblance," Lilly agreed. She patted him on the shoulder. "Could happen to anybody. Forget it. . . ."

At the front desk, a distinguished-looking guest who might have been a captain of industry was just checking in.

"What was all that fuss about?" he asked the desk clerk.

"I don't really know, sir," the young man replied. "The President's coming in tomorrow, and there's been all kinds of strange activity."

Signing "James Carney, San Jose," Mitch Leary said, "I can imagine. I'm here for the President's visit myself."

Leary had just been handed his room key and arranged for his bags to be taken up when a voice called out behind him.

"Finally we meet!"

Leary, caught off guard, turned and faced a red-haired, heavyset man with a round face and wide smile.

"You *are* Jim Carney?"

Leary gave the overbearing asshole an affable smile. "And you must be Pete Riggs."

As they grasped hands, Riggs—impeccably dressed in dark brown suit with yellow-and-gold tie, in the clothes-horse manner of a slightly overweight man seeking to compensate—beamed and shook his head, as if awestruck in the presence of one James Carney.

"I was starting to wonder if you really existed," Riggs said, grinning like the idiot Leary imagined him to be.

"Oh? Why's that, Pete?"

"All those generous checks to the Victory Fund. I was starting to think you were an angel sent from Heaven to help the President."

"Oh, I'm no angel, Pete."

Riggs slipped an arm around his new best friend. "Well, then—how about a drink, you devil?"

Taking him by the elbow, the glad-handing Riggs ushered Leary over to a bank of glass elevators.

Leary glanced around, taking the place in. The modern catacomb nature of the place surprised him; poor choice to protect a President in, he thought, happily. Tonight he'd have to prowl around, some. Do some low-key reconnaissance.

"When does the President arrive?" Leary asked.

"Just in time for the dinner tomorrow night," Riggs said. "Oh—that reminds me . . ." He stopped for a moment, and dug in his inside suit-coat pocket. "Here. . . ."

An engraved invitation for "An Evening with the President."

Leary's smile was genuine. "Why, thank you, Pete."

"And I got you a *great* seat. Practically front row."

"Couldn't ask for more."

They boarded the elevator, which took them up five floors over the cavernous open lobby, until the car emerged to traverse the exterior of the building, providing an expansive view of the city—including, on a rooftop below, some cops talking with some men in suits who Leary was sure were Secret Service.

"Tell me, Jim," Riggs asked. "What exactly *is* Microspan Corporation?"

"Pete, I didn't come to L.A. to talk business—I came to meet my President."

"Yes, and I can't wait to introduce you. . . ."

Soon Riggs and "James Carney" were seated in the revolving lounge, thirty-five stories above downtown L.A.—not that you could see it under the veil of smog. Two tables were pushed together, and Leary was sitting with other fat-cat friends of the President, everyone but Leary tossing down the drinks, getting well and truly sloshed.

"You know what the problem is?" Leary was saying to the inebriated CEO of a Silicon Valley computer software company. "We're thinking about the next fiscal quarter, while the *Japs* are thinking about the next quarter *century* . . ."

"Fuckin' A," the CEO said.

A voice Leary immediately recognized as Frank Horrigan's spoke behind him: "Mr. Riggs?"

Frank Horrigan, standing right fucking behind him! An exhilarated Leary, as giddy as any of these drinkers, hid behind the calm facade—the dark-rimmed glasses and black toupee and black moustache and brown contact lenses and dark tan and Brooks Brothers suit—of James Carney.

Riggs got up, taking his drink with him, and joined Horrigan, moving just a bit away from the group.

"Who's *that* guy?" the CEO slurred.

"Secret Service agent," Leary said matter-of-factly.

Leary pricked up his ears; his hearing was excellent—that much, about his CIA file, was accurate.

"Mr. Riggs," Horrigan was saying, "I understand you're in charge of the California Victory Fund dinner tomorrow night?"

"That's correct."

"Do you know everyone attending the dinner?"

"What do you mean?"

"I mean, do you know them personally?"

"I sure do."

"Could you look at these photos?"

"If you insist."

"Ever see any of these people?"

Leary was quivering with excitement, but knew it didn't show. Surely photos of him were among the stack Horrigan was showing Riggs; probably including computer-generated projections of what he might look like in various disguises. Had they stumbled on to one resembling James Carney?

He'd soon know.

"No, no, no," Riggs was saying impatiently. "I never saw any of these people. Look, I went through all of these with another agent yesterday. I'm happy to cooperate, and I know you got the best interests of the President at heart—but honestly, we're trying to do something positive, here."

"Yes, sir."

"And, frankly, Agent Harrigan—"

"Horrigan."

"Frankly, this is starting to border on harassment. If you'll excuse me."

Leary half-turned to glance at Horrigan, who glanced over at the table.

And nodded politely at the drunken assemblage of fat cats, tucked his tail between his legs and went on about his business.

"Another drink, Jim?" Riggs was asking, his moonlike face, a little booze-reddened at the moment, hovering over him.

"No thanks," Leary said. "I have some work I have to do in my room this evening."

"Thought you said you didn't come here for business!"

"Oh, I didn't. Strictly pleasure. But, you know what they say—no rest for the wicked."

Later, in his hotel room, Leary watched the TV with interest as KCOP reported on the Secret Service agent who, "thinking he spotted a potential assassin," had roughed up a bellboy. The entire sorry spectacle was preserved on tape for God and the world to see.

"Might not have your job tomorrow, Frank," Leary told the television with a *tch tch,* as in his lap, arms motionless, hands nimble, he assembled pieces of his resin composite gun. "Then where's the challenge for me?"

When he was finished, he checked his watch, made a note of the time it had taken on a scratch pad, then broke the weapon down and started again.

26

•••••••••••••••••••••••••••

Horrigan stood at a window in the darkened Presidential Suite, which tomorrow night would be home to a real President, curtain drawn back so he could contemplate nighttime downtown L.A.

He'd seen the report on KCOP; he knew the kind of trouble he was in. But he wasn't thinking about that.

He was thinking about two men he'd known; married men with wives and children, who had been in the employ of their government. Who had done their country proud. Who had been slain by assassins.

One was famous, a household name, a dead President.

Another would fall through the cracks of history, just another dead cop.

Both were tragedies he had let happen.

He was also thinking about a third man who had been in his government's employ who, if he had not done his country proud, had at least done its bidding. Mitch Leary's tragedy was ongoing, but Horrigan intended to see that it ended soon.

"Frank?"

It was Lilly.

Standing in a distorted rectangle of light that fell through the door she'd opened, Lilly looked pretty, and pretty businesslike, in her silk blouse and navy skirt and heels.

"What are you doing up here, in the dark?" she asked, gently. "Agents Bates spotted you on the monitor and thought we had an intruder, for a minute. . . ."

"Sorry."

She joined him; he didn't look at her, but he liked feeling her presence there beside him.

Her voice was warm, concerned. "Frank, what are you thinking?"

"Just trying to figure out what else I can do. To make sure we don't have another tragedy on our hands tomorrow."

She touched his sleeve. "You know, I kinda think between the LAPD, the FBI, the sheriff's deputies and the United States Secret Service, we can handle anything that might come along. There's two hundred and twenty-nine people protecting Traveller tomorrow."

Horrigan's smile was a thin line. "That's a lot of guns. If Leary gets off a shot, we're liable all to buy it in the crossfire."

Faint sounds of traffic, from below, leached in.

"Frank . . . Bill Watts just called."

"Don't tell me. He saw KCOP. Knows about me and my bellboy pal. . . ."

"So does Traveller." She sighed, patted his shoulder. "I told Bill you did what any one of us would have. I know, I was *there*—but he seems to think we're *all* 'overwrought.'"

Horrigan snorted.

"Harry Sargent apparently had a shit fit," she said.

"He'd jump on any chance to discredit me," Horrigan said flatly.

"Anyway. General consensus of the people whose opinions count, which does not include yours truly, is that you're a press liability, here in L.A. So—you're to report to San Diego tomorrow."

He glanced sharply at her.

She didn't avert her gaze; she was sympathetic, but professional as she said, "You're to assist the PI on the advance, there."

He turned back to the window. Down on the street, a siren cried.

"Just like that," he said.

"It's not just *you* against Leary, Frank—have a little faith in the rest of us. We'll get him. We'll stop him."

He put a hand against the window, for support; it felt cool. Then he turned to her and said, quietly, "For thirty years I've endured idiots on their bar stools with their cockamamie theories about Dallas. . . ."

The word stopped him: *cockamamie*. He could see Al's *you're insane* expression, hear his laugh.

He swallowed, went on.

"It was the Cubans, it was the CIA, white supremacists, oil-rich Texans, the mob. There was one gun, there were five guns."

She stroked his sleeve.

He looked out at the city, but didn't focus, making it a glittery black blur. "Christ . . . it was such a pretty day. Rained all morning, before the sun came out. So the air was almost cool. That first shot . . . I thought it was a firecracker."

The memory of it still confused him.

Haltingly, he told her, "I turned and saw him . . . saw that he was hit. I don't know why I didn't react faster—I should have. I should have been running, running to him, running toward him, but . . . I just couldn't believe . . ."

He swallowed thickly, looked at her; her face was lovely, her expression tender.

"Lilly, if I'd reacted faster, I could've taken the shot."

She arched a gentle eyebrow. "You wouldn't be here today."

"That would be fine with me. Maybe Jack would be." He shook his head. "Maybe Al would be, too."

She slipped her hand in his and squeezed.

"Lil—it's a hell of a thing to have to live with."

"I know. I know."

"Would you . . ." He swallowed again. "I'm not sure I ought to be alone tonight."

She nodded.

They went back to her room. Slipped out of their shoes, deposited their Secret Service guns and other gear on opposite end tables, crawled onto the bed and fell asleep in each other's arms.

He started to have the Dallas dream, but he must have been talking in his sleep, because he heard her saying, "No! No. You're here, with me, everything's fine, Lil's here," and her hand was ruffling his hair and stroking his face, and he dreamed he made sweet, tender, passionate love to her.

But it wasn't a dream.

27

By late the next morning, in the unloading lane in front of the United Airlines terminal at Los Angeles International Airport, Horrigan was grabbing his tan canvas carry-on bag out of the backseat of a green unmarked Secret Service Plymouth Reliant.

Checking his watch, he leaned in the car window and asked, "You got the number of the San Diego Field Office?"

Agent Chavez, recruited to be Horrigan's chauffeur, smiled genially and said, "Sure—ukulele."

That took Horrigan slightly aback. "Ukulele? What are you talkin' about? You're too young to remember Arthur Godfrey."

Chavez's eyes were bright as he explained, with an odd mixture of pride and embarrassment, "It's a memory trick I picked up in the Army. That's how I remember the number—you know, a seven-letter word for seven numbers. Just push U-K-E-L-E-L-E."

"You're spelling it wrong," Horrigan said. "It's U-K-U."

"Maybe so." Chavez shrugged. "But the number is U-K-E. Easy to remember."

Horrigan smiled wearily and shrugged. "If you say so. Thanks for the lift."

Inside the airport, lugging his heavy carry-on, he muttered, "Ukulele," mildly amused as he headed for his gate. Along the way, he stopped at a pay phone, to check in with the San Diego office. Using his credit card, he pressed in the area code and began punching in U, then K, then paused to think about the spelling.

He hung the phone up, got out his notepad to write UKELELE down; the page he flipped to was one where he'd been fooling around with anagrams and a backward spelling of SW SKELLUM LA. The phrase itself was written in large letters in the middle of the note page.

"Hey," he said to no one.

Seven letters in "skellum." If LA stood for Los Angeles . . .

He pressed in the letters S-K-E-L-L-U-M on the touch-tone dial. He tapped the notepad with his pen, anxiously, as the phone rang in his ear.

Finally, an efficient female voice said, "Southwest Bank."

He circled the SW.

Southwest.

The voice said, "May I help you?"

"You already have," Horrigan said. "What's the address there?"

As he hurried toward an exit, he caught sight, on a TV in a mini-lounge, of the President descending the steps of Air Force One, trailed by agents including Bill Watts and Matt Wilder. Time was fleeting.

So was Horrigan.

In his room on the twentieth floor of the Bonaventure, Mitch Leary, sitting on the edge of his bed, carefully unscrewed the metal tip of his lucky rabbit's foot, the part that held his keys. This revealed two hollowed-out areas inside the lucky piece.

Into the holes, Leary inserted two nine-millimeter cartridges. Then, quietly humming his favorite Beatles song, he screwed the metal cap back on, keys jangling, sealing the bullets within, hiding them away.

"I'm sorry," the attractive Customer Service teller said, her big blond sprayed hair making Horrigan have to crane his neck to see past it and her gold hoop earrings, to the computer screen where she was scrolling through accounts. "Nothing on any of the names you gave me."

He'd had her try Mitch Leary and several variations, as well as aliases listed in the CIA file.

Behind the wall of teller cages, several other employees, a few more women than men, were gathered around Horrigan and the Customer Service teller at her computer. They were passing around photos Horrigan had given them—photos and computer alterations of Leary.

Horrigan turned to them as they looked through the photos, murmuring among themselves, shrugging, shaking their heads negatively.

"Try to imagine him in a disguise," Horrigan offered. "A hat, a wig—a mustache, maybe."

The woman at the computer, whose name was

Marge, had already leafed through the photos.

"I *know* I never saw him here," she said, "but then, I've only been working here a couple of weeks."

"Who was in charge of new accounts before?"

The murmuring behind him ceased, as if somebody had shut it off with a switch. He turned and saw lowered eyes; fallen faces. Somehow, for some reason, his question had thrown a ghastly pall on the proceedings.

"Is there something wrong?" Horrigan asked. "Who opened new accounts before Marge, here?"

A plump brunette with too much compensating makeup stepped up to speak timidly. "Pam. Pam Magnus did."

"Where can I find her?"

"She . . . she's gone."

"Gone?"

"Somebody killed her."

Horrigan, stunned, stepped forward and placed a hand on the teary-eyed young woman's arm. "She was murdered?"

The young woman nodded painfully, gazing over at a picture, in her teller's window, of another slightly overweight blonde—a snapshot of her ice skating. Her smile was glowing. A nice girl.

"That's her?" he asked.

The teary-eyed teller nodded.

He went to the framed photo, picked it up; looked closer: Pam Magnus wore a sweatshirt in the snapshot, a sweatshirt with a big, distinctive, flourished *M* on it.

Wasn't that the symbol of the Minnesota Twins?

He felt the blood draining out of his face. "Pam was from Minnesota?"

The teary-eyed teller nodded.

Some people die simply because they're from Minneapolis.

"Where, exactly?" he asked.

In his hotel room, Leary sat on his bed, inserting the disassembled pieces of his resin composite gun into special pockets sewn into the cummerbund he would wear, tonight, with his tuxedo.

Then he went to a chair by a window and sat, wired and yet calm, looking out at Los Angeles, at rooftops below him where police snipers lurked. He smiled.

"For what good it will do you," he said softly.

As Marge searched computer files, Horrigan used the phone in the Customer Service teller cage.

"Lilly," he was saying, "I got hold of the homicide detective working the case, and he says the girl . . . actually, *two* girls, her friend was killed, too . . . were taken out commando style."

"Commando style?"

"He reached right out and twisted their necks like twigs. Broke them."

Marge, at the computer, glanced at him and swallowed. The tearful coworker didn't overhear; she'd already gone home, a wreck.

"Traveller is adamant about going through with tonight," Lilly said, working her voice up over a din in the lobby, her voice crackling over the cellular phone. "Unless we can prove Leary is on-site, Harry Sargent won't cancel the dinner."

"The proof might be a dead President."

"Frank, you *have* to go on to San Diego! For your sake and mine. We're ready for Leary, here. If Watts and Sargent find out you're still in town . . ."

"Lil, I love you dearly, but I'm hanging up now."

"Frank!"

He cut her off, turned back to Marge, and said, "We know what the last day Pam worked was. We can start with that date and work backwards."

Marge shook her head, no, and said, "Problem is, Agent Horrigan, we don't log accounts by the dates they're entered."

"How do you?"

She shrugged. "Name or number. It's going to take some time to do the search."

He touched her shoulder, smiled gently. "This is going to sound corny, Marge, but your President's life depends on it."

Her nod was somber.

"I want you to fax me the list as soon as possible," he told her, and scrawled on a note sheet the number of the Secret Service Communications suite at the Bonaventure.

"You got it," she said. "Even if I didn't vote for the guy."

Dusk was falling.

From his hotel room window, Leary could see tiny toy-soldier police manning miniature barricades below. The streets for blocks around had been cleared of pedestrians and vehicles. But for the toy soldiers, the world was a deserted playground.

And now here it grandly came: the Presidential motorcade, antenna flags waving, so many cars. He had counted fifty, watching on TV. Sad that security precautions had denied the President a cheering audience along the sidewalk sidelines.

But the President did have an audience, didn't he? An important audience in a high window. Who, after all, was more important than the President's assassin? Wasn't Leary the man who would accompany him, hand in bloody hand, through the pages of history?

Checking himself in the mirror—his tux looked perfect, the cummerbund with its precious hidden pieces just a part of the pasta-fed potbelly he'd given himself over the last weeks—he sighed with satisfaction.

He plucked his engraved invitation off the nightstand, stopped to allow his fingertips to drift over the card's raised surface, stroking sensually for a moment, and went off to have dinner with his friend, the President.

It would be dark soon.

Traffic on the Santa Monica Freeway was gridlocked. In the back of the taxi, Horrigan had broken open his revolver, checking his ammunition.

"Go up on the shoulder," he told the Hispanic driver. "Drive like hell."

"I can't do that, mister," the cabbie said.

"Do what I tell you," Horrigan snapped.

The cabbie, glancing in his mirror, must have seen Horrigan checking his gun, because he changed his mind and pulled up onto the shoulder and hit the gas, kicking up dirt and gravel.

Horrigan slipped his gun in his shoulder holster and buckled his seat belt.

He *couldn't* be late.

He was the show.

28

· ·

When the Presidential limousine pulled up in front of the Bonaventure Hotel, Lilly Raines—dressed in a black, tuxedo-like pants suit with white silk blouse, her black scarf like a tie around her collar—was waiting at the curb.

"Command Post Raines," she said, speaking into her cuff-mike. "Arriving."

The agents who'd been running alongside the limo now formed a human ring around the stopped vehicle, their fingertips touching slightly, as a tuxedoed Bill Watts jumped out of the front seat, to open the President's door.

The President beamed, waved, to a small, controlled crowd, TV crews jostling for the best angle; the print media's cameras clicked and whirred, as Lilly led the President—with Bill Watts one small step behind—onto the red carpet laid out before the hotel entrance. Along the way, Peter Riggs, chairman of the California Victory Fund, with the hotel manager and various officials—all wearing their designated yellow lapel pins—greeted their President with gushing enthusiasm.

Other vehicles were emptying out, and the Presidential retinue was following: Harry Sargent, a military aide, the White House press secretary, the Marine lieutenant colonel entrusted with the attaché case of doomsday nuclear codes, and of course the black bag–carrying Presidential physician, as well as Matt Wilder and other agents.

Everything was under control, everything going smoothly, as Lilly guided the procession inside.

"So far so good," she thought, but in her heart of hearts, much as she hoped he was on his way to San Diego right now, she wished Horrigan were here.

On the second floor of the hotel, just outside the doors opening onto the Catalina ballroom, men in tuxedos and ladies in gowns waited in line to pass through the freestanding frame of an airport-style metal detector under the steady gaze of Secret Service agents, themselves in formal wear. None of these loyal, often generous campaign contributors seemed to mind—it only added to the excitement. Drink glasses were clinking, conversation hummed, laughter echoed.

Among these wealthy friends the President was getting a little help from was Mitch Leary, his tuxedo bearing the green lapel pin that designated him one of these honored, cleared guests. Adjusting his glasses on the bridge of his nose, he passed calmly by an Hispanic agent who was thumbing through a stack of photos clipped to a clipboard.

Probably crazies they're on the lookout for, Leary thought, with an inner smile, knowing that if his picture were in there, it wouldn't resemble his James Carney persona.

Leary took his place in line with that computer software CEO he'd met last night in the revolving lounge; the guy wasn't sloshed tonight, but he was high, all right—on the thought of meeting the President.

"I'm as excited as a little kid," the CEO confided.

"Oh, it'll be a night to remember," Leary said.

The CEO set off the buzz of the metal detector; he laughed nervously, stepped back through, placed his keys in the tray the agent provided, and tried again. No problem.

When Leary stepped through, the alarm again buzzed. He removed his lucky rabbit's-foot key chain, dropped it clangingly into the tray the agent extended like an offering plate at church. Leary stepped back through, tried again, no buzz; the agent handed him his key chain, and "James Carney" entered a chandelier-flung ballroom, elegantly arrayed for the banquet.

An American flag draped the wall behind the dais; its podium bore the Presidential seal. The Chief Executive would face a sea of round tables, linen tablecloths set with crystal and china, appointed with red-white-and-blue floral centerpieces. Uniformed waiters circulated with trays of brimming champagne glasses. By a small dance floor area, a tuxedoed orchestra was playing an elevator-music medley of Beatles songs.

I wonder if they take requests, he thought.

Finding his place card, he took his seat at a table on the aisle down which the President, no doubt, would make his way to the dais. Perfect. *Thank you,*

Pete Riggs. Those campaign contributions were money well spent. . . .

As the room filled up, Leary began removing the pieces of his resin composite gun from the pouches in his cummerbund. His hands moved deftly beneath the tablecloth; he had practiced and practiced this, and it paid off: his arms seemed to hang loosely at his sides, not betraying the swift, precise movements of his hands below the table.

"Ladies and gentlemen," a voice boomed, and Leary almost dropped the nearly assembled weapon.

It was the public address system.

"The President of the United States!"

The crowd rose to its feet, exploding in impassioned applause; Leary—snapping together the last component of his gun—lagged only a few seconds behind. He slipped the assembled pistol between his knees and stood and applauded wildly, his face ecstatic with the nearness of the President.

The orchestra was playing a syrupy, quavery version of "Hail to the Chief," but you could barely hear it over the applause and whistles and stomps and cheers, as this distinguished group of contributors turned into a rowdy if friendly mob.

The applause lasted a long time, but it trailed off, people sitting back down, Leary included, as the President, good ol' Pete Riggs right on his arm, worked his way up the aisle with the dais their eventual destination, stopping to "press the flesh" with these well-moneyed constituents along the way.

The more you'd spent, the more time you got.

And Leary had spent enough to rate a nice long introduction and handshake; Pete Riggs would see to that. . . .

Leary fumbled with his lucky rabbit's-foot key chain; he'd been calm up till now, but his heart was starting to race, the adrenaline starting to flow. . . .

The President and Riggs were followed by White House Chief of Staff Sargent and some people Leary didn't recognize, including a Marine lieutenant colonel. And, of course, the usual escort of Secret Services agents—including that blond bimbo of Horrigan's—but they didn't look too alert. Their guard was definitely down, Leary noted with pleasure and relief. Not so obsessively protective, in such well-to-do company.

He unscrewed the metal tip from the key chain, shook the bullets out into his palm, but one bounced off, and onto the floor!

Stay cool, he told himself. *Stay calm.* . . . .

The President and Riggs were walking right toward him.

He dropped his napkin, dipped down to pick it up, plucked the bullet off the floor as well; no one noticed anything—all eyes were on the President.

Two tables away, Riggs was introducing the President to one of the fat cats from the get-together at the rooftop lounge yesterday, a patriotic citizen who'd offered a waitress a C-note for a blow-job. Hurray for Old Glory. Under the table, Leary slipped the first slug into the gun. Above the table, these movements were undetectable. Then the second bullet was snugged in place.

A small commotion attracted Leary's attention.

Horrigan!

The agent had come up the aisle, behind the President, and was conferring frantically with several of the agents, including that blonde bitch of his. Leary sneered. Too little, too late.

He shut the chamber on the weapon, and draped his hand—and the gun—with a linen napkin. The President and Riggs were approaching, smiling.

"James Carney" stood, his face frozen as he extended the napkin-covered hand.

When Horrigan came bounding into the Bonaventure lobby, he was breathless and sweat-soaked, buttoning up his shirt, which fit tight, his carry-on bag still in hand.

"Hold this!" he told Robert Stermer, behind the bell captain's desk, tossing the bellboy the canvas bag. Stermer's eyes went wide at the sight of the agent.

"Yes, sir!"

He headed across the vast lobby, past cops and agents—all of whom recognized him—and hopped onto the escalator that would take him to the second floor and the Catalina ballroom.

He would have sprinted up the steps, but an Hispanic guy in a tux was blocking him—then he realized it was Agent Chavez, reading as he rode up, flipping through some sheets on a clipboard.

Horrigan tapped him on the shoulder. "Did a fax come in for me?"

"Frank!" Chavez looked back saucer-eyed. "Are you out of your mind? What are you doin' here? Watts is gonna have a shit fit if he sees—"

"I said, did a fucking fax come in for me?"

They stepped off the escalator into the second-floor lobby area, where a few more tuxedoed agents stood post.

"Yeah, one came in just a few minutes ago." Chavez held up the clipboard, pointed to the top sheet. "I was just gonna take it in to Agent Raines—"

"Give."

But Horrigan just took, grabbing the clipboard out of Chavez's hand.

Chavez was shaking his head. "Jesus, Frank—you're really losin' it."

"Where's Traveller?" Horrigan asked, running a finger and his eyes down the page, which was a list of the half a dozen new accounts opened by Pam Magnus at Southwest Bank of Santa Monica on the final day of her life.

"Well, he's in the ballroom. The fund-raiser's about to start."

Horrigan moved in that direction, still tracing a finger down the sheet, then he stopped—his feet, his finger, his eyes. Chavez almost bumped into him.

"Microspan Corporation . . . James Carney," Horrigan read. "You got the guest list printout on that clipboard?"

"Sure."

"Give!"

Horrigan took, ran his finger down the list of campaign contributors and stopped at "James Carney, President, Microspan Corporation."

"The bastard's *here*," he told Chavez, and then he ran through the metal detector, gun under his shoulder setting it off, into the ballroom, down the aisle, toward the President, who in the midst of agents and a few others, was making his slow way to the dais, shaking hands, making nice. . . .

Harry Sargent turned to see what the bustle was about, and scowled at the sight of Horrigan, saying to Bill Watts, "What the hell is he doing here?"

"I don't know," Watts said, and broke away and met Horrigan in the aisle, blocking the way, like a toll taker. Lilly came running, too; Horrigan wondered if her look of concern was for him or the President.

Watts began: "Who gave you permission to—"

Horrigan cut him off: "Leary's here. He's using the name Jim Carney. . . . He's a goddamn campaign contributor!"

"You're *not* part of this detail—"

Horrigan grabbed Watts by the tux collar. "Get me a goddamn seating chart!"

Watts was a prick, but he wasn't stupid. Horrigan knew he'd made his point; the dark-haired agent nodded, and waved for another agent to come over.

In the meantime, Horrigan moved past the Presidential party, to the front of the room, putting his back to the dais, where he could get a full view of the enormous banquet hall, raking the crowd with his eyes. So many faces . . . so little time. . . .

Where was that fucking seating chart?

That asshole Pete Riggs was walking the President to the next table, where a group of supporters were getting to their feet. The one nearest the President was a tanned, distinguished-looking executive type with glasses, a slight potbelly, and—

Why wasn't he smiling?

Everybody else in this entire goddamn hall was beaming, and this guy had an intense expression, and a napkin over his hand. . . .

"*Gun!*" Horrigan yelled.

But in the clamor of the room, it got no immediate response. He saw the other agents reacting to him, but haltingly, Wilder, Watts, Lilly looking around, not seeing anything. . . .

The President hadn't even heard him, apparently, and was holding out his hand to Leary, smiling, just a few yards away from the man who had come to kill him.

Horrigan had never run faster. Maybe nobody ever had.

He ran and he threw himself through the air like goddamn Superman and leapt in front of the President, as Leary fired, the napkin catching fire, the President getting shoved back, the bullet catching Horrigan squarely in the chest.

And he went down.

29

The shouts and screams of the crowd, as the dignified, formally attired guests dove under tables and scrambled for the exits, provided shrill accompaniment to the lightning response of Watts, Wilder and five other agents, who immediately formed a human wall around the President. Agents, some of them disguised as waiters and waitresses, were suddenly everywhere, all at once, handguns materializing from under jackets, Uzis emerging from nylon bags and attaché cases. Agents barked into cuff-mikes, alerting the world outside the banquet room of the madman in the tuxedo.

The President's would-be assassin overturned the big nearby table, dishes and silverware tumbling off in a clattering cacophony, keeping agent Lilly Raines from getting a clear shot at the bastard.

Watts and Wilder had already lifted the President up under his arms and off the floor, sweeping him along, racing him within a moving wigwam built with the bodies of agents willing to give their own lives for this man they were protecting, taking him into and through the kitchen, and onto a service elevator, to the basement, where the President was rushed to his limo, around which an armed police guard stood watch, and where he was virtually shoved inside by Watts.

"That agent," the President, breathless, said to Watts, who was glued to him, both men sweating as if in a sauna, not a backseat. "He saved my life. What was his name?"

The Presidential limo flew out of the hotel's underground garage, with the follow-up car and two police cars bumper-to-bumper behind.

"That was Frank Horrigan, sir," Watts said. "A hell of an agent."

Horrigan, nearly unconscious from the impact of the close-range nine-millimeter gunshot, was down on his side on the carpeted floor, when a hand grabbed him, yanking him up, tearing the front of his shirt, revealing the white Kevlar bulletproof vest that had saved his life. If he hadn't taken time to put it on, in back of that cab, he would be dead now, not dazed. . . .

The chaos of the room ringing in his ears, he was trying to keep his feet under him, and wondering who had helped him up, when a hand jerked the revolver from the shoulder holster under his arm, and he realized he wasn't being helped at all.

It was Leary—making a human shield out of him, shoving the barrel of Horrigan's own gun in his neck.

"Get back!" Leary was shouting. "Keep away!"

The room was spinning, faces, distorted faces,

swimming before his eyes, as Leary dragged him back, back against a wall. Horrigan could see Lilly's face, lovely face, tortured face, as she and other agents leveled their guns on Leary, not daring to fire.

"I'll scatter his fucking brains!" Leary was screaming. "So help me Christ Almighty!"

Horrigan breathed slow and deep, though it hurt his bruised—or were they broken?—ribs to do so, getting his wits back about him, the dizziness easing up even as the nose of his own .38 dug deeper into his neck, Leary's left arm coming from around behind him to hug him in a bizarre embrace, Leary's left hand still clutching the squarish cream-colored gun.

Harry Sargent was standing with a hand on the front of his tux, drenched in sweat and tears, his breath rapid, possibly hyperventilating; his black-bagged eyes locked onto Horrigan, and were frankly regretful. An agent came up and pulled Sargent back, off the line of fire.

Lilly and the other agents, guns in hand, were closing in gradually on Leary, like lion tamers cautiously approaching an escaped king of beasts. But this time it was the lion who had the whip and chair. . . .

Sliding along the wall, Leary dragged Horrigan to the doorway, the pressure on the gun in his neck never letting up; then, looking in his tuxedo like a demented headwaiter showing a guest to his table the hard way, Leary walked Horrigan out, into the second-floor lobby, where agents and cops were everywhere, the press corps swarming, too—TV cameramen and still photographers alike jockeying for position, trying for that Pulitzer-Prize camera angle.

Perched high on landings in the four stories of the open lobby above them were snipers; Horrigan saw them, and a sweating Leary saw them, too.

"You're finished, Mitch," Horrigan said.

"Shut up!" He pressed the gun even tighter in Horrigan's neck as he walked him, shoved him, over toward the bank of elevators.

"The President's safe by now, Mitch," Horrigan said. "Elvis has left the building."

"Shut up, Frank!"

Leary, his back to the elevators, Horrigan serving as his human armor, slapped the Up button savagely, like a big bug he was swatting. All the noise and activity seemed to be spooking Leary: flashbulbs popping, TV crews scrambling for shots, Lilly shouting orders to agents . . .

"Here's that attention you craved," Horrigan managed, though it killed him to speak, his ribs ached so. "Don't blink—here's your fifteen minutes of fame. . . ."

"Will you *shut up*, Frank!"

Horrigan could see a sniper above, taking position, looking for an opening; Horrigan tilted his head to one side, to give the marksman a better shot, but Leary glanced up, got wise, and ducked down behind his prisoner.

"That was naughty, Frank," he said.

Leary's composure was coming back; not good.

Elevator doors opened on an empty car, and Leary—keeping the .38 snout dug in the flesh of Horrigan's throat—backed inside, with his captive in tow.

No sooner had they stepped inside the booth of glass than the wall behind them exploded with Uzi fire, fragmenting the glass on all four sides, and Leary spun his prisoner around, taking cover behind him. No bullets hit either of them, but the shattered glass rained in, more of it hitting Leary than Horrigan, one king-size sliver gashing the gunman's cheek.

Leary, still clutching Horrigan from behind, gun still in Horrigan's neck, cream-colored weapon in the other hand, elbowed the button for the twentieth floor. The elevator—which consisted now of shards extending from the skeleton of its supporting steel cage—rose out of the lobby, gliding up into the outside world, alongside the exterior of this towering building with its many mirrored windows, into the chill night air, the lights of the city spread before them like glittering jewels tossed on black velvet.

Suddenly Leary released Horrigan, shoving him against the other side of the car, where the agent bumped against the steel railing, almost tumbling over, but catching his balance just in time. Luckily his hands had gripped where the glass was completely gone; a few inches over, and he'd have cut his palms to ribbons.

With the heel of his left hand, Leary punched the Emergency button.

The elevator jolted to a stop.

The jarring halt intensified the pain in Horrigan's side, and made him gasp for air, and the deeper he breathed, the more it hurt. His face ran with sweat, possibly with tears—he wasn't sure.

Across from him, against another half-wall of this skeletal elevator car, Leary leaned against the rail, his tuxedo looking rumpled, his face similarly streaked with sweat and maybe tears but also blood, from the gash. With the back of his free hand, Leary brushed it away, smearing his knuckles red.

He was watching Horrigan closely.

The wind was blowing through the exposed car, whistling through and rustling the remnants of the glass walls. It was like holding your ear to a seashell—if you added the wail of police sirens and shouting below.

But that was below. Up here, in this half an elevator car, facing a madman who held Horrigan's own gun on him, the agent felt suddenly, strangely, tranquil.

At peace with himself.

At rest.

Then he winced with pain, and Leary said, with what seemed like genuine concern, "Are you okay, Frank?"

It hurt to talk, and Horrigan winced as he spoke. "No, you moron. You busted my goddamn ribs."

Leary's soft laugh seemed in harmony with the whistle of the wind; glass shards shivered like ice. "Still have some spirit left in you, don't you, Frank? Hope you're up to playing our final round. . . ."

"Game's over," he said. "President's safe."

"But you're not. Are you, Frank?"

Here in his own little world, in this broken box of a universe suspended over the city, Leary too seemed tranquil, comfortable, at home. With a twisted smile, he bent at the knees and placed the cream-colored weapon he'd fired at the President on the glass-littered floor of the car. A foot away from himself, more or less.

Then reaching out toward Horrigan, he placed the

.38 revolver on the floor as well, about a foot away from the agent.

Leaning back, he gestured to the guns, as if inviting Horrigan to go for his.

Horrigan was looking at the cream-colored gun. "You made that thing? No metal for the detectors to pick up—model-building techniques . . ."

Quietly proud, Leary nodded.

"How'd you get the bullets past 'em?"

Leary smiled again, dipped a hand into his tuxedo pants pocket and tossed the rabbit key chain over to Horrigan, who caught it, examined it, unscrewed its metal cap and saw the slots for the bullets.

"Pretty slick."

"Thank you, Frank. I don't take a compliment from you lightly, you know. What about you? How did you know about James Carney?"

Out of the corner of an eye, Horrigan spotted two LAPD SWAT sharpshooters taking their positions on the adjacent roof. He needed to keep Leary distracted, so they could pick him off.

Chattily, he said, "The phone number—Skellum. I spent the afternoon at Southwest Bank, closing out your account."

"Ah. Nice detective work."

Horrigan gestured with the rabbit's foot. "Mostly luck."

"It plays a role, Frank. Luck. Fate. Kismet."

"You're not going to sing, are you? I'm gettin' a little airsick up here as it is."

"What made you think James Carney would be at the fund-raiser?"

Horrigan started to shrug, thought better of it, the way his ribs felt.

"Your sense of irony, Mitch. Your favorite Beatles song. You hid yourself among the friends of the President, didn't you?"

Leary's smile was affectionate, his tone warm. "We played a hell of a game, didn't we, Frank? I don't think anybody appreciates us the way we appreciate each other."

Now Leary caught the sharpshooters from a corner of his eye, and he turned to them, raising his hands, displaying his lack of firearms.

"Smart move," Horrigan said. "Now they won't shoot you, at least not right away."

Hands still up, he said, "Right. They think I'm surrendering."

"They're wrong, aren't they?"

"You know they are, Frank. You know me so well."

Leary lowered his hands and faced Horrigan. He said, "Are you afraid to die, Frank?"

"No."

"That's either admirable or sad."

"I suppose it's both."

"Why . . . don't you have *anything* to live for, Frank?"

"My daughter."

"You hardly see her."

He thought. "I like to play piano."

Leary shook his head. "That's not enough."

"How would you know? Do you play piano?"

"Are you in love with her, Frank?"

"Who?"

"You know—Lilly Raines. Your Lincoln Memorial date."

"That's a little personal, Mitch."

"Everything is personal between us, Frank. Does she give your life meaning?"

"It's early yet. But I'll tell you what *does* give my life meaning."

"What, Frank?"

Horrigan gave him the coldest smile he had; and he had some.

"Stopping you."

That froze Leary, for a moment, then he shrugged, and nodded.

"That's nice, Frank. I'm happy for you."

Horrigan eyed the .38 on the glass particle–strewn floor, inched his body slightly closer.

Leary did the same.

Then they both leaned back, and Leary began to sing the Beatles song—track 2 on the CD. His voice was soft and melancholy and oddly tender.

Leary was still singing when Horrigan plucked the gun from the floor, a movement as quick as it was deliberate, as smooth as it was sudden, and he fired.

Simultaneously, Leary went for the homemade gun, with its one remaining shot, and his gun went off just as Horrigan's did, two overlapping thunderclaps that shook the night and the remaining glass in the elevator.

Horrigan rocked back, tagged in the upper left arm.

But Leary took his in the chest—about where he had hit Horrigan, earlier—only Leary wasn't wearing Kevlar.

The force of the close-range gunfire knocked Leary

back, against the rail, over the rail, and his flailing arms caught first the rail itself, but slid off, yet somehow his two hands were gripping the lip of the elevator floor, fingertips pressed into bits and pieces of glass, but gripping nonetheless.

And this time it was Mitch Leary who was dangling off a high place.

The smoking revolver still in hand, Horrigan—the pain of his shot-up arm not registering yet—went over and looked down at his adversary, whose face was contorted with pain, whose white dress shirt was soaked with blood as he strained to maintain his hold. . . .

Horrigan put his gun away, and leaned over and out and offered his hand.

Despite his pain, Leary managed one last, faint smile, shaking his head ever so slightly, declining the offer, and then either his strength failed, or he just let himself go, because the fingers loosened and he dropped and he plummeted, looking up at Horrigan, smiling gently, as he grew smaller in Horrigan's vision.

Leary crash-landed, on his back, on the steel supports of the roof over the glass lobby below.

Horrigan stood looking down at the twisted corpse of a twisted man while the wind whistled through the broken glass around him; in the adjacent shaft, another glass elevator was suddenly next to his, and in it were Lilly and two SWAT team guys with automatic weapons.

Lilly put her hand on the glass, pressing it there, like the wife of a prisoner on visiting day. Her face was both tortured and relieved—an expression he could identify with. . . .

They looked at each other for a long moment. Smiled. Nodded.

Fuck irony, he thought. *Give me love every time.*

He pushed the button for the first floor, and as he rode down, wind ruffling his hair, he got one last close look at Leary and his strange smile, the would-be assassin sprawled on the rooftop, as the elevator descended, leaving him behind, just a bloody mess for somebody other than Horrigan to deal with cleaning up.

In the lobby, a bloodied but unbowed Horrigan exited the elevator under his own steam, though paramedics, cops and his fellow agents swarmed around him. He knew he was in shock, but knowing that didn't lessen it, and he felt the hand of one of the paramedics, guiding him.

"We gotta get you on that gurney," a young paramedic was saying.

"This isn't another gag, is it?" he asked.

The pop and flash of camera bulbs, the shouting, the sirens, it all blurred his eyes, his ears, and he wondered if he would pass out. As the paramedic walked him toward the gurney, Horrigan suddenly found himself confronted by a grinning Harry Sargent, with a still photographer in tow.

Photo op, Horrigan thought.

"A job well done, Frank," Sargent said warmly, enthusiastically, sticking out his hand. "The President wanted me to tell you, personally, that— "

"Sorry if I overreacted again, Harry," he said, ignoring both Sargent's hand, and the photo op, allowing the medics to usher him to the gurney, where he promptly passed out.

30

Several days later, Horrigan, fresh off a jet, his left arm in a sling, walked through the arrival gate at Dulles Airport with Lilly on his right arm, letting her carry both their carry-on bags. They looked casual in their sweaters and slacks, and did not expect the swarm of media, the bright lights of TV crews or the machine-gun questioning of that same KCOP newswoman who had witnessed his misidentification of the bellboy back at the Bonaventure.

"Agent Horrigan? Why are you retiring from the Secret Service on the eve of your biggest triumph?"

He stopped to answer the question. Why fight it? This was *his* fifteen minutes.

"I hate desk work, I'm too old to run alongside limousines, and thanks to you guys making me famous, I'm worthless for undercover assignments."

Another reporter asked, "What are your plans?"

"Play a little piano at the corner bar. Subsist on

my pension until I marry this woman here, and then live off her."

"Have you set a date?"

"That's classified," he said. "And if the Secret Service knows how to do anything, it's keep a secret."

That was all he gave them.

Sam Campagna met the couple just after they worked their way through the press throng. "How you feeling, Frank?"

"I been worse."

Campagna's eyes smiled. "Really taking my advice and retiring?"

"You bet."

"Well, it better wait till after next week."

"Why's that?"

"The Secretary of the Treasury's got some going-away presents he wants to give you—the Secret Service Medal of Valor and the Treasury Department Exceptional Service Award."

Lilly clutched his good arm; he smiled sideways at her, and she beamed at him, her pride in him sweetly apparent. These were the highest honors their profession could present. Hell of a career capper.

"Well, what about the damn President?" Horrigan asked gruffly. "I didn't save the Secretary of the Treasury's life, you know."

Campagna grinned, jerked a thumb over one shoulder. "He's sent his limo to pick you up."

"Good," Horrigan said. "You know how partial I am to public transportation."

Soon he was sitting in the spacious backseat of the Presidential limo with Lilly plastered against him, her hand on his thigh.

"How about a night on the town?" she asked.

"We've got a car and a driver. . . ."

"Capital suggestion, my dear," he said, in his lousy W. C. Fields impression. "But let me go freshen up first."

This was her first glimpse of his apartment, and it was a literal eye-opener. She surveyed the scene of the disaster, answering his "Make yourself at home" with "I'm not sure that's possible."

She helped him change the dressing on his wound in his bathroom, which also lacked a woman's touch. Or a human's touch.

"Living with me is no picnic," he told her.

"Oh, I think we're compatible."

"How can you tell?"

"I know people," she said. Her smile was wicked. "That's what they pay me for."

He was getting dressed, pulling on his trousers, while she was poking through his jazz CDs. On the table by his chair, the answering machine's light was blinking furiously.

"Hit the button on that, will you?" he asked her.

She did, the machine rewound, and a familiar, wispy whisper of a voice came on.

"Hello, Frank."

Leary.

Horrigan zipped his pants, and walked into his little living room, eyes narrowed. Lilly was sitting up, hand to her lips, face frozen with shock.

"By the time you hear this, Frank, our game will be over. The President is, most likely, dead. And so am I. Did you kill me, Frank? Who won our game? Not that it matters. . . ."

She rose and went to his arms, and he patted her back comfortingly, saying, "Help me get into my shirt. With this damn arm, I need a little help. . . ."

She was doing that, while Leary's voice continued: "Between friends, it's not whether you win or lose, but how you play the game. But, now, the game is over, and I worry about you, Frank."

Horrigan tied his tie himself, but had to have Lil snug it for him.

Leary was saying, "I worry that, with me out of your life, you won't have any life left at all. It's time to get on with your life, Frank, but you have no life to get on with. How sad."

"Chinese?" he asked.

"Definitely!" She helped him into his sport coat. "After supper, can we make a sentimental stop?"

"Sure," he said.

Leary said, "You're a good man, Frank. And good men, like you—like me—we're destined to travel a lonely road. . . ."

"Fuck him," Horrigan said, and the machine was still playing when they went out, arm in arm.

They didn't hear Leary say, "I wish you all the best, Frank. I hope, in years to come, that from time to time, you'll think of me—and that, when you do, it will be with a certain fondness. Good bye . . . and good luck."

After supper, they sat together on the steps of the Lincoln Memorial, leaning against a column, Horrigan's good arm around Lilly, her head snuggled against his chest, warming each other.

It was a beautiful night in Washington, D.C., but there was a chill in the air.

Exceptional Service

A number of friends around the country served as impromptu resources: Captain Richard J. Tracy, Chicago PD, and publicist Barry Axler shared insights and expertise about Presidential visits to Chicago; artist Terry Beatty revealed arcane secrets of the model-kit collector subculture; while others provided location information: Ann Fleener, Minneapolis; Bill Mumy, Los Angeles; Barb Lutz, St. Louis; and Jan Grape, San Antonio. Only I, however, am responsible for any inaccuracies in these pages.

A special thanks to my wife, Barbara Collins, who helped assemble and assimilate research material.

These books provided background: *The Dangerous Assassins* (1964), Jack Pearl; *How the White House Really Works* (1990), Jack Sullivan; *Howard Baker's Washington* (1982); *Protecting the President* (1985), Dennis V. N. McCarthy with Philip W. Smith; *The Secret Service in Action* (1980), Harry Edward Neal; *Washington DC Touring Guide*, Michelin (1991); *Washington, the Capital* (1981), Robert Llewellyn.

I would also like to acknowledge editor Elizabeth Beier, for solid support, as well as my agent Dominick Abel.

Finally, thanks to Jeff Maguire for his first-rate script, and to Clint Eastwood for inspiration.

About the Author

Max Allan Collins is a two-time winner of the Private Eye Writers of America "Shamus" award for best novel, for his historical thrillers *True Detective* (1983) and *Stolen Away* (1991), both featuring 1930s Chicago P.I. Nate Heller. He is also author of an acclaimed series of historical police procedurals about Eliot Ness, most recently *Murder by the Numbers* (1993).

He scripted the internationally syndicated comic strip *Dick Tracy* from 1977 to 1993, is co-creator (with artist Terry Beatty) of the DC comic-book feature "Ms. Tree," and has scripted the *Batman* comic book and newspaper strip.

A singer/keyboardist with rock bands since the sixties, he currently records and performs with both Seduction of the Innocent (in California) and Crusin' (in his home state, Iowa).